Princess For The Pack

OMEGA FOR THE PACK
BOOK THREE

LAYLA SPARKS

SAPPHIRE INK PUBLISHING LLC

Omegaverse Terms

A few things to know regarding the omegaverse world. The people in the omegaverse display a canine or wolflike behavior. Some books involve shifting into wolves. This series will have minimal shifting.

Here are some terms that will be helpful to know (*note: these definitions pertain to my stories):

Omega: A female or male who would often have multiple partners to help them during heats. Usually has a particular scent that alphas find very appealing and unable to resist.

Beta: Like a normal human but in the wolf world

Alpha: Top of the food chain, and they gravitate to omegas. They also have a scent to attract omegas.

Delta: Ferocious and deadly, typically guards and second in command to alphas

Slick: Secretion from the privates

Heat: A period where an omega needs to mate - akin to ovulating in human females.

Knot: When an alpha mates an omega— and the base of the penis swells, locking the alpha and omega in place

Rut: Alphas can go into rut phase, similar to heat. Sometimes an omega's heat will bring it on.

Scent blockers: Can come in pills or as a cream. Blocks an omega scent from attracting alphas.

Heat Suppressants: Stops an omega from going into heat

Prologue

Lyra

My alpha fathers were taking on a new omega. I couldn't believe my eyes when she finally walked into our palace, confirming all the rumors that my fathers had not been loyal to my mother.

Perched atop the staircase, I watched my three alpha fathers greet their new omega into the throne room.

At least, I was sure she was an omega.

She was young, with fiery red hair and oval eyes. They hugged her in turn, and I felt sick to my stomach. They had taken in a new omega from the last Omega Ball.

This was a nightmare in the making. King Saku, the oldest of my fathers, passed away three months ago, and the rest of the fathers had already started to act on their lust.

My mom was still wearing black and mourning my oldest father. Saku was the only one who held the family together like glue, with everyone trying to seek his wisdom.

The family bond was over once he passed away.

The distance between my fathers and my mother, Queen

Ophelia, lengthened day by day. My fathers pounced like lions on the next omega they saw without their brother's guidance just because my mother could not bear any more children.

I watched, shocked and dismayed, as the omega kissed them all on the lips. Her hips swayed seductively as she walked to each of them in turn, and bile rose in my throat.

My fathers were supposed to be comforting my mother and not blatantly kissing this omega for all to see.

Making my way down the stairs, I decided to destroy this little party. They all looked at me when my heels clicked on the throne room floors, announcing my presence. They quickly distanced themselves from the red-haired omega.

King Armon, now the oldest of my fathers, smiled upon seeing me. He was tall and lanky with a long gray goatee. He had taken over as king after Saku passed away.

"Daughter, meet Vanessa," he said, gesturing to the new smirking omega. "We didn't expect you'd be here at this hour."

"Saku died. Not Mom," I hissed. Then I turned to the omega. "My mom is still alive and married to them. So why don't you pack up and go back home, bitch?"

My fathers gasped at my audacity, but I didn't care.

Vanessa's eyebrows rose, but her smile was still stuck on her face. She had a permanent clown face with thick red lipstick.

One of my fathers jumped in, trying to cover for me.

"Lyra's still grieving, and she's only nineteen–just a kid. Let's get to know each other some more in the other room."

"Of course," said Vanessa in a silky, thin voice, following the alphas deeper into the palace.

I felt like throwing up. *Weren't my dads too old to keep up with a horny omega?*

I sighed loudly, and my bodyguard walked over to me. Luke was my friend and confidante while growing up at the castle. He was the only person in the world besides my mother, whom I trusted. He was tall and had a body made of rock, and he was wearing his official black and red royal guard uniform.

"You should check on your mother," he said in a low voice. "Forget what they're doing here, my princess."

"You're right," I said. I had no idea if she'd seen the brand-new shiny omega yet. "Do you know where she is?"

I had to tell my mother the news. My fathers had already found a new omega to breed with.

"She's in the library."

"Okay," I said, heading off toward the library. I walked down the vast hallways, my heels echoing down the chamber.

My mother was sitting in a large armchair that was too big for her as she sobbed into her hands. The upper half of her body was wrapped in a large black shawl.

"Mom?" I said, wrapping my arms around her in a hug. "I'm sorry."

She didn't say anything as she quietly sobbed into my shoulder. Burning tears pricked my eyes. She had most likely seen everything that transpired in the throne room.

If my fathers could act like this and discard my mother to the side, how could I trust anyone?

I vowed never to fall for any alpha, no matter how nice he was. Because if one day, I couldn't have babies as my mother did after her miscarriage, it would be easy for an alpha to leave.

And that wasn't going to happen to me. Not if I could help it.

One

LYRA

"We, the Bloodhound Pack, wish to ask Lyra's fathers for her hand in marriage," said the leader of a pack of alphas in the throne room.

I almost laughed out loud.

The pack of three looked desperate and miserable, standing there waiting for an answer.

"Well, Lyra?" asked one of my fathers. Armon turned to me as he sat on the throne. He had the king's crown on his head, made of gold and wrapped in silver. "Would you like to give these respectable alphas a chance?"

I squeezed both sides of my chair in frustration.

"Of course not," I said, gritting my teeth.

"Why not?" asked Vanessa snidely. She sat at the end of the line in the throne room. My mom wasn't here and constantly avoided the new omega if she could help it. I had never seen them in a conversation without one of my fathers involved.

"Because a home-wrecker like yourself can mess up my marriage," I said.

She gasped. Armon clapped twice to divert everyone's attention from the drama brewing between Vanessa and I.

"I apologize, Bloodhound Pack. You may take your leave," said Armon, rubbing his temple in frustration. "My daughter doesn't seem interested at this time and has much growing up to do."

Growing up? I was nineteen, for fuck's sake. And what the hell was he frustrated about? I was the one who had to get marry complete strangers to fulfill my destiny of growing the Royal Pack. Mom had locked herself up in her room for days and refused to come out. It had been two months since my fathers took on this new omega, and Vanessa was already fucking pregnant, gloating as she rubbed her small tummy for show.

She was just a home-wrecker. Pure and simple.

I watched as the Bloodhound Pack left the throne room, the leader with his hat in hand. I couldn't care less.

"Well, it's time for me to go," I said. "My friends are waiting at the café."

"You may go," said Armon, shaking his head in disapproval at how I acted.

I ignored him as I stepped off the platform, nearly tripping as I held onto the long, red-clothed table in front. As I walked, my dress swished behind me on the gold and red carpet. I met my bodyguard, Luke, at the door. His light-brown hair ruffled in the wind, and his stark green eyes focused on me.

"To the café?" he asked.

"Yes, I need to get out of here," I said, getting into the black limo in the front. Luke sat next to me as the driver started the car.

"May I ask what happened?"

"My fathers are trying to get me married off again," I said. "I'm not just some omega to get married and settle down. It's not happening. I want to do amazing things for Howl's Edge and be the lady for the people."

"If you keep ignoring every pack that comes for your

hand, you might get old and lonely," said Luke. "At least give them a chance. You can still be great while settled down."

"Why don't you talk about yourself?" I shot back. "You're almost forty years old and haven't settled down yet."

"Settle down. I didn't mean anything by it," said Luke, taking my hand in his. When his large, warm hand enveloped mine, a flicker of electricity shot through me, and I quickly pulled my hand away.

What the hell?

He must have felt the same because he looked straight ahead, his pale cheeks reddening. He had been my bodyguard for so long that there was no way I could have feelings for him. I suddenly noticed how close his thigh was to mine. And how his body made the car feel small all of a sudden.

My breathing quickened, and I felt like I was hyperventilating.

He was an alpha, and his nostrils flared as he smelled my aroused scent. The smell of peaches filled the car but had a slight burn to it.

"I'm sorry," I whispered.

"Don't be," said Luke in a low voice. "Just calm down, okay? I know you're upset about an arranged marriage in your future, but it shouldn't be so bad."

Thank goodness he attributed my scent to feelings of anger instead of arousal. And there was no way I would tell him I felt a spark between us.

AT THE CAFÉ, I sat with my friend and my cousin at a table while Luke stood outside the door, pacing up and down the small road. The Café de Lune was a quaint little establishment nestled in the heart of Howl's Edge. It was a popular gathering spot for omegas. The atmosphere was warm and inviting. The walls were painted a soft, buttery yellow, and the floors were dark, polished wood. The plush velvet seating and the natural sunlight made it my favorite hangout spot.

"You keep staring at him," said Beth with a slight smile as she sipped her latte. She had long black hair and a hooked nose. Even though she was a beta, she was one of my best friends growing up. Her mother was a maid at the palace, so we essentially grew up together, even though it was frowned upon for a princess to be friends with a beta. My mother knew about it but didn't say anything.

"No, I'm not," I protested, quickly blowing the steam off my coffee.

Ever since Luke held my hand in the limo, I couldn't help but wonder, and my thoughts were going into forbidden territory. My face warmed, and I took a sip of the rich coffee. I had to squash the intimate thoughts immediately.

"Look at how red her face is," said Yasmeen, fixing the red polka-dot bandana around her forehead. She liked to dress in loud colors with her matching polka-dot red dress. She was my cousin on my fathers' side. "Lyra, do you think you can do my makeup?"

"Of course," I said, pulling my makeup satchel from my purse. It was handy and ready. I loved doing makeup and looked forward to it when anyone wanted their face done. I started laying out the eyeshadow colors, lipstick, and eyeliners on the table. "Did you bring your own foundation?"

"Yep," said Yasmeen.

As I dabbed the foundation on Yasmeen's nose, Beth wouldn't stop asking questions about Vanessa.

"Is Vanessa, like, totally okay with your mom still being there?" she asked.

"She doesn't give a shit," I said, trying to blot the foundation just right. "If she could talk to my mom every day just to brag, she would love it."

Over the past two months, Vanessa floated around with her long red hair and bossing servants around. But, of course, my fathers thought she was a charming omega because she didn't do any of that stuff while they were around.

We were suddenly interrupted by loud yelling coming from outside. The screams were earsplitting.

"What the heck is going on?" said Yasmeen, half her face done with makeup.

I threw all the makeup back into my bag, running to the door in my silver heels. Luke was standing just outside the café doors, watching something down the road across from us.

"What's happening?" I asked Luke breathlessly.

"Get inside," ordered Luke with fear in his voice, his face white.

I caught sight of ten males with their fangs showing and fur running down their arms. They looked like a mix between a wolf and a human, but they were not fully shifted. What the hell? They were attacking people and trashing market stalls. I saw one bite into an old lady's neck and fling her to the ground like trash.

Horror filled me. I'd never seen destruction to this level before on Howl's Edge. We prided ourselves on having a peaceful island. They looked like feral animals that I'd never seen before.

"The Wild Wolfmen are here," said Luke, barely gasping out the words. My fathers had been keeping them under control for so long, but the day had come. Luke grabbed my hand and we rushed into the café. I saw my friends hiding under a table, their hands over their mouths as they watched. The cafe owner shut the door and began barricading it with tables.

But they were too late.

The door smashed open, and Luke quickly covered me with his body behind the coffee counter. We were kneeling behind the counter, and I felt Luke's body pressing over me and enveloping me as he tried to protect me. I heard windows smashing and people screaming.

"My friends," I whispered, trying to get up, but Luke held me down.

"My job is to protect you. Only you," he growled into my ear as he tightened his grip around me. His strength was steel as I tried to push him off, but it was fruitless.

The screams grew louder, and my heart pounded out of my chest.

"Please, Luke, we need to help my cousin and my friend," I stressed.

"Stay behind me, then," he ordered. When he finally lifted off of me, I ran around the counter and saw a scene of utter chaos.

The windows were smashed, and guests were lying on the floor covered in blood while the Wild Wolfmen fed on their bodies. Tables and chairs overturned, broken glass, and spilled food everywhere.

The smell of blood and fear hung thickly in the air.

"Help!" screamed Yasmeen, her face red and her bow askew. One of the Wild Wolfmen was stalking towards her, a leer on his face.

"Stop!" I screamed, trying to rush to them, but Luke held me back by my arm. We were instantly surrounded by Wild Wolfmen who were covered in fur. From up close, their fangs dripped with slobber as they made grunting noises and barked at us. Their stench was unbelievable, like unwashed bodies and dead animals.

"Fuck," said Luke, holding a small pistol in his hand. He turned around in circles, not sure where to shoot. We were surrounded.

The door slammed open, and everything stopped when he entered the cafe.

He was a giant with long, curly black hair and a large scar over one eye. His black shirt was ripped in several places, and his biceps were bulging. He glared at everyone in the room. Finally, his eyes turned to Luke and me in the middle of all the chaos. My heart beat faster upon seeing him. He wasn't hairy and fanged like the creatures around us.

"It's the Princess Omega," he growled, his eyes on my tiara. He lifted a hand, and the Wild Wolfmen backed away from us. "Hello, Princess."

I was staring daggers at him. So, he was the leader of these half-wolf monsters terrorizing the city.

"Get out of my city," I said with all the command I could muster in my voice.

"Not until I finish my job here," he said, his face turning up in a sly smile.

"Take your men and leave at once," Luke said in a stern command, training his gun on this giant of a man.

This mountain of a man didn't give off alpha vibes but something else. His scent of ashes burned through the room, overwhelming me. I looked over at my cousin, Yasmeen, and she was kneeling on the ground with a Wild Wolfman hovering over her. Following my gaze, the leader of the Wild Wolfman made his way over to her, ripping off her bandana.

She was staring at the ground, trying not to look at him.

"Look at me," he commanded, lifting her chin up.

My heart pounded with fear at what he was going to do. Goosebumps rose from every inch of my skin.

"Please," she whispered, but he wrapped his fingers around her throat. Tears dripped down her face.

"No!" I shouted, running to them when Luke let go of me momentarily. I grabbed the leader by the arm. Everyone gasped, and the leader looked at my hand on his arm like I was just a nuisance.

"What makes you think I'll listen to you, little princess?"

he asked with that sly smile. His hand was still around Yasmeen's throat. She was gasping for air, and I could hear it. My chest hurt just listening to her.

"I'll do anything," I said. "Whatever you need. Do you need money from the Royal Pack?"

Then he cocked his head to one side, pondering what I'd just said. I was hoping he wasn't thinking of something devious. I've never seen him before, and his presence was intimidating.

"No. You will marry me, then. Me and my second-in-command alpha. That will ensure your fathers will never attack my people again," he said, squeezing Yasmeen's throat tighter. "Then I'll take my men, and we'll be gone."

Marry him?! Luke touched my elbow.

"Don't do it, Princess," he whispered.

"That's fine," I said quickly. I couldn't think. I was watching Yasmeen's face turn red. "Release her."

He released his hold on her, and Yasmeen fell back on her heels, rubbing her neck. I sighed in relief. Next, I'd have to worry about this marriage problem.

"Take us to your palace," he said. "We can tell the Royal Pack to fuck themselves. We're making this wedding official."

"And you promise never to come back to the city?" I pressed. At the same time, I needed to be careful. He could set the Wild Wolfmen on another killing spree at any time.

"Are we doing this or not?" he growled, grabbing my arm.

"Yes," I said, feeling his large fingers squeeze my upper arm, digging into my skin.

"Then take us to your fathers, little princess," he said, his eyes on mine. I could tell this guy didn't trust easily and didn't like to be tricked. There was no way to back out of my decision.

I was going to have to bring him to the palace whether I liked it or not.

Two

My heart raced as I walked toward the palace while the leader of the Wild Wolfmen followed closely behind. He had driven his truck the whole time behind our limo. Reporters for the Howl's Daily swarmed me while we made our way to the palace. Luke was blocking off the reporters from getting to me, his muscular arms holding them back.

"Princess, princess. Is it true you're marrying the leader of the Wild Wolfmen?" asked one of the reporters.

Ignoring them, I stared stonily toward the palace that was only a few feet away. The palace was made of gleaming white marble, with tall, stately columns that stretched up to the sky. It was built on a large piece of land, and it was surrounded by a high, wrought iron fence that was lined with sharp, pointed spears. The Royal Pack guards surrounded us as we walked forward, blocking me from the leader of the Wild Wolfmen.

I didn't dare look back at him or his sidekick alpha walking next to him. I had caught a glimpse of the alpha earlier. He had black hair that was slicked back and a smooth, clean look to him. But there was something about his eyes that scared me.

Soulless. Empty. Like serial killer eyes.

I was freaking out inside with every step. How the hell would I get out of this arrangement? I already promised them marriage. It was the only way to save everyone.

"Get back," Luke commanded the reporters as we entered the palace. I stepped onto the carpets, leading my entourage toward the throne room. When I pushed the door open, revealing the five thrones, I saw my fathers chuckling and drinking tea.

Upon seeing us, Armon dropped his glass, which shattered all over the floor.

"What is the meaning of this?" He stood up from his throne, nostrils flaring.

Vanessa was sitting off to the side, watching the proceedings curiously. My heart pounded even harder as I stood in front of them. I caught sight of my mom sneaking into the throne room from the library, her hand over her mouth as she saw the leader of the Wild Wolfmen in the same room as us.

"Armon," I said. I always addressed my fathers by their first names. It was weird, but it was how they wanted me to address them since I was a child.

He held up a hand, and I went quiet.

"How dare you walk into my city and my palace?" Armon addressed the leader of the Wild Wolfmen. "Get out of here before I kill you myself, Kodan."

Kodan walked around me, facing my father head-on.

"Your precious city is surrounded," said Kodan. "I only called them off because your daughter offered herself in marriage to me."

"No," said Dravin, who was another alpha father of mine. He had a huge belly as he sat on his throne. "We will kill you before we let our daughter marry you. And Voss, you're here too. You coward."

He was addressing the alpha sidekick of Kodan's.

"How am I a coward?" asked Voss, his silky smooth hair shining under the lights. Instead of a ripped shirt and jeans like Kodan was wearing, Voss wore a nicely pressed suit and tie. A nicely dressed murderer.

"Every year, you attend the ball. If I knew you were in cahoots with the Wild Wolfmen, you would never have stepped foot in my home," said Dravin, shaking his head in disappointment. His lips furled in disgust.

"Daughter, we need to talk," said Armon, turning his attention away from Kodan. "Before any big decisions are made."

"Take all the time you need, King," mocked Kodan, crossing his big arms across his chest.

My breathing accelerated with fear and nervousness. My family wasn't happy about this.

I followed Armon, Dravin, and my mother into the library, with Luke following close behind. My youngest alpha father, Arther, remained in the throne room, keeping an eye on Kodan, along with several guards standing silently around the throne room.

IN THE LIBRARY, I sat at the table surrounded by my family. Luke stood at the door, giving us a semblance of privacy, but his eyes were on me with his arms crossed in front of him.

"Don't do this," my mom pleaded, grabbing my hand.

"He is our biggest enemy," said Armon. "Daughter, you don't have to do this. We will find another way or even declare war on him."

"I can do it," I said, pulling my hands away from my mom. "You always wanted me to get married. So why is this any different? I'm saving our people."

"Our daughter always does the opposite of everyone," sighed Dravin, his head in his hands.

"No, I don't," I argued. Out of all my fathers, I was the closest to Dravin, and it was easier to talk to him. But ever since Vanessa came into the family, I didn't talk to my fathers except for an occasional greeting.

"This is different because Kodan is not an alpha," said Armon.

"So?" I countered. I wasn't sure what Kodan was. But he didn't give off the alpha vibes when I was standing next to him. The air around him felt different, and his scent was harsher.

"He is a sigma," said Armon, scratching his mustache.

"What's a sigma?" I asked. It sounded like a stupid question, but I honestly didn't know. I didn't know much about them because they were even rarer than omegas like me.

"They are lone wolves," said Armon. "Like the big bad wolf we never talk about. They are naturally aggressive and don't do well in a domesticated household. He's not the family man that I want for you."

Oh, whoa.

I wasn't sure about this. I've never seen or heard about sigmas in my life, considering I lived at the palace and my fathers always fought off the Wild Wolfmen. It was an ongoing fight that never ended.

"If I back out now, it'll start an all-out war," I said.

"She's right," said Luke, clearing his throat. My eyes widened. He usually didn't speak up during family meetings. "If she ends up marrying the guy, I'll make sure she's safe."

"I can live with that if you go with her," said Armon, rubbing his forehead in thought. "If anything happens at all, come right back home. Okay?"

"I will," I said.

Don't you worry, Dad. If he's crazy as hell, I'm running right back home.

"Time to arrange everything, then," said Armon. "I will speak to Kodan and let him know our final decision."

Wait, what? Everything was happening too fast. Couldn't he wait a couple of days? While Armon spoke to Kodan in the throne room, I could feel my heart pit-patter in my chest out of nervousness and indecisiveness.

We sat quietly in the library while Luke shuffled around the room. Every tick from the large grandfather clock above sounded like a boom. Dravin was scribbling notes on a piece of parchment while my mom munched on little chocolates from the candy bowl on the table.

"What the hell am I doing?" I said out loud as my mom passed me a piece of chocolate candy.

"You're saving the kingdom," said Mom. "That's what we should tell ourselves."

"So, you're okay with this now?" I asked.

"After thinking about it, this is the only time you've volunteered to get married," said Mom proudly. She had always wanted me to settle down. I dropped the candy on the table, shaking my head.

"I'm forced into it," I said.

"No one forced you, honey. You decided to save your people."

I didn't want thousands to die when it was just me who had to get married. I was going to be pressured into marriage regardless, even if it wasn't to Kodan.

At least this way, people didn't have to die.

Luke opened the door for Armon, and he stood solemnly before us in front of the bookshelves. He didn't look happy, and his eyes were filled with unshed tears. Damn, I didn't know my dad cared that much, considering how he treated my mother.

"It's final," he said. "The wedding will be tonight."

"Oh, my," said Mom. "We have to start getting you ready, Lyra. We only have a couple of hours left until sunset."

Without warning, Kodan strolled into the room, and Luke grabbed him by the arm.

"It's okay," said Armon, and Luke released him with a growl.

"Sheesh," said Kodan, shaking his head. "I came to talk. I'm family now."

Kodan sat across from me, and I finally got a good look at him. Even though the scar above his eye was intimidating as hell, his green eyes were playful and held an air of mischievousness.

"What is it?" I asked.

"You're not shy at all," he said with a half-smile. The curls of his long black hair almost covered his eyes. He pushed his hair back with one hand, his gaze on me not flinching. Not looking away. "Are you ready to marry me, little princess? Are you regretting your choice?"

My heart jumped at being called that again. I didn't want to be his little princess. Yet at the same time, the feral side of me wanted it.

I've held back those feelings for so long, taking heat suppressants religiously every day, waiting for the one day I could throw them away. But I didn't trust him. I needed to keep them.

"I'm ready," I stammered, the bravado from earlier vanishing. "But I have one request."

"And what is that?" he leaned forward on his hands, and the table suddenly became small.

"I want Luke with us to make sure I'm safe."

"Your bodyguard?"

"Yes."

"Well," he said, intertwining his fingers over the crystal snack bowl. "There's one condition."

"Okay?" I said, my heart lifting.

"You will only be allowed to be around males you are married to," he started. My heart began to sink at what he was going to say next. "You can have him around. But under the condition that he marries you tonight, along with myself and Voss."

Oh, my god.

I looked over at Luke, and he gave me a slight nod with a serious look on his face. He was okay with this idea! I started biting my fingernails, the glitter pink nail polish falling on my lap. The only way I could stay safe was to have Luke around. There was no way I was going alone to a foreign society with this sigma.

No way in hell.

"That's fine," I said bravely. "Are you okay with that, Luke?"

"I am," Luke said without a shadow of a doubt as he gazed at me. "I'm not letting you go alone in this."

My heart beat a little faster with both males watching me. Warmth fluttered in my center.

"Interesting," said Kodan, rubbing his chin with his weathered fingers. "Another alpha in my pack. I'm not very fond of alphas, y'know?"

"Well, you're going to have to deal with me," said Luke, standing taller.

"Let's get you ready," said Mom, grabbing my hand.

"Alright," I said, standing up and gathering my dress around me while Kodan and Luke stared daggers at each other.

"PUT HER HAIR UP," said Mom. While the maid worked on my hair, Vanessa was doing my makeup. I closed my eyes as Vanessa applied the eyeshadow on my eyelids.

Vanessa. Yep.

She had to help, at Armon's orders. Obviously, I didn't want her here, but I wasn't going to be the one who started the fight. She knew how to do makeup even better than me since our makeup artist was out, and this was last minute. While the maid attacked my hair, Vanessa poked me in the eye with the makeup brush.

"Ow, what the heck Vanessa," I sighed, shutting my eyes tight.

"Sorry, the brush slipped," she said. I didn't believe her for a second. "Are you nervous about getting married?"

"Of course I am."

"Don't be," said Vanessa. Who was she to give me advice? "He might be just what you need. Someone to break through your perfect little shell."

"He's the complete opposite of me," I said, taking offense at being called sheltered.

"Yeah, Kodan's definitely rough around the edges," breathed Vanessa.

"Alright, back off before you get too excited," I said.

"Ooh, someone is already possessive," laughed Vanessa. I seethed inside. "Makeup's done."

I opened my eyes and looked into the mirror in front of me. The simple silver eyeshadow with the black eyeliner made my blue eyes look sultry. Not too bad. The pink lipstick and the blush complimented my skin with a little highlight on my button nose. My blond hair was done in a nice updo, curls framing my face.

"I like it," I said. "Thanks."

"I know, I'm the best," said Vanessa. "Well, I'll see you at your wedding even though you and your mama never talk to me."

When she left, my mom finally spoke. She absolutely refused to talk to Vanessa or join the conversation if I was talking to Vanessa.

And understandably so.

"Your hair is perfect," she said, patting the stray hairs down.

"What am I going to wear?" I said, panicking and looking at the sunset outside. It had taken forever to get my hair and makeup done after my shower. I made sure to shave every part of my body too. Who knew what was going to happen on the wedding night? Would all the males just pounce on me? Ravish me until the morning? I grew nervous, especially since Luke was involved. He was going to be one of my husbands by tonight.

My mom brought out a long cream dress from my canopy bed, which I didn't even notice. She must have put it there while I was in the shower.

"My old wedding dress," she said proudly. It was clean cut in the front with no sleeves, and it was stunning, with a row of white petals going down on each side. I held my breath as I softly touched the fabric.

"It's so beautiful," I said.

"You better wear it before I throw it away," said Mom. "You know exactly how I feel about your fathers."

"I know, Mom," I said, pulling the dress on over my white bra and slip. She helped zip me up, and we both looked in the mirror. My hair piled high on top of my head made me look regal, with little blond tendrils of hair framing my face.

"Here is the jewelry, my queen," said the maid, handing my mom a box. She opened the box, and I gasped when I saw the diamond set inside.

"I want you to think of me when you wear this," Mom said, pulling out the diamond-studded choker necklace.

"This is too much," I protested, not wanting to take her most precious jewelry. I choked up as I looked into the mirror after she put it on me.

"You are the light of my heart and for the kingdom," said Mom. "You deserve every single piece and more. I pray that you find love with Kodan and his pack. As your mother, that is all I wish for."

"Thank you, Mama," I said, hugging her, tears in my eyes. She believed that I could do this. That I could somehow bring peace between the warring factions. I thought about the sigma and the two alphas waiting for me at the altar.

Trepidation and fear swirled inside me.

KODAN

"Are you sure of this, Kodan?" asked Voss.

We were standing at the end of the altar, the officiant in front of us, holding a book in one hand. I still wore my scrapped-up shirt, while Voss looked more than ready for the occasion in his suit. The dumb ass bodyguard of the princess stood next to Voss, his body facing away from us. Luke, was it?

I knew he was only here for the princess, but he had better strap in and be a loyal pack member. If I saw any sign of disloyalty from Luke, I was more than ready to kick him the fuck out.

"I'm damn sure," I said, roughly pushing my hair away from my eyes. I needed to cut my hair one of these days. Maybe the cute princess could help me out. "Once we're married into the Royal Pack, it'll grant us immunity from random attacks. They won't want to harm their own princess."

"That's smart," said Voss. "It gives us more power too. Are you planning to stay loyal to this omega? Or are you going to keep sleeping with the Wild Wolf ladies?"

"Ha," I chuckled. It had been years since I last slept with someone. And my cock couldn't wait to consummate this marriage. "Those days are over, Voss. Now, where is our bride?"

As soon as I said it, the double doors opened slowly at the end of the room.

In the front, leading the procession, was King Armon.

Behind him, the princess followed, clutching her fathers' hands on either side of her. She looked so delicate under her white veil. So petite and small. She kept her head down as she walked towards me. Her tough shell had clearly vanished at this moment. When she looked up at me with those sky-blue eyes of hers, my cock hardened underneath my jeans.

I was going to ravish her tonight.

Four

LYRA

I tried to keep calm and relaxed as I stood before Kodan, Voss, and Luke. Even though my heart was pounding like crazy, I kept my face neutral.

The room was full of guests invited at the very last minute by my parents. They had managed to show up, despite the same-day ceremony. I had quite the nosy family members. When the officiant started to speak, my heart hammered in my chest.

This was getting all too real. It wasn't fun and games.

I was going to be a wife today.

And if the sigma wanted to be intimate with me, I had to give in to him. I had never slept with anyone before. I've tried exploring myself when I couldn't help it, but I was the most inexperienced omega he could ever get. So I hoped he was patient, which seemed highly unlikely.

Kodan's eyes hadn't left my face as soon as I walked in. Luke had an even expression on his face, but he gave me a small smile and a wink when I made eye contact with him throughout the ceremony. Voss looked rattled and shaky, his eyes never meeting mine. His face was pale for some reason. Maybe he didn't want to marry me.

This was going to be a disaster of a wedding.

My stomach clenched as I thought of the wedding night. The sigma looked like he wasn't waiting for anyone. From the side of my eye, I didn't dare look down–I could see the hint of his erection pressing against his pants. He hadn't even thought to change into a fancier outfit.

This wedding wasn't important to him at all. I was just going to be a wife. That was all there was to it.

The more I stood there, the more I wanted to run away. Before I could change my mind, the officiant had already reached the end.

"Do you, Kodan, leader of the Wild Wolfmen, promise to protect and love Princess Lyra of the Royal Pack?"

"I do," said Kodan, his eyes focused on mine.

My stomach cinched with butterflies of nervousness. Then the officiant turned to me next.

"Do you, Princess Lyra, agree to marry Kodan of the Wild Wolfmen? To have and to hold until death do you part?"

My heart was pounding hard, and I couldn't say anything at first. I was tongue-tied.

"I...I do," I whispered.

"Could you repeat that?" asked the officiant.

God, this was mortifying.

"I do," I said, and a smug smile crossed Kodan's face. What did he think was so funny? Jerk.

"Kodan, Voss, and Luke, you may all kiss your bride," announced the officiant.

Kodan approached me first, slowly lifting my veil over my head.

My heart was beating fast as his hand curled around the back of my neck, pulling me roughly toward him. He was like the feral version of an alpha as he took my lips in his, kissing me soundly. I had no choice but to surrender to my new sigma husband, allowing him to kiss me. His lips were firm but soft against mine, and I could smell his slight scent of ashes up close. He wasn't anything I'd been around before. My inner omega still responded to him as it would with an alpha, getting warmer with his touch, feeling his essence flow against mine.

He pressed his body against me, and my body heated in response allowing him to envelop me. I didn't want this kiss to end; his fingers tightened on my neck. I heard him let out a slight groan when I pulled my face away.

When he finally released me, I was nearly limp and breathless.

∼

Luke

WATCHING Princess Lyra enjoy the sigma's kiss bothered me. He was the enemy of the Royal Pack and somehow muscled his way in.

As I stood there, watching them, I couldn't help but wonder if she regretted marrying me.

I didn't regret marrying her, though.

Because the truth was...I had been obsessed with her ever since she came of age. Keeping it a secret was the hardest thing in my entire life. But keeping her safe was my top priority.

She looked stunning in her long white veil flowing behind her as Kodan dipped her body in a kiss. Her dark eyelashes fluttering in desire caused my cock to stir. Princess Lyra was every alpha's fantasy on Howl's Edge. Countless times, she'd refused offers of marriage. She was picky and hated all alphas, especially after what her own fathers did. I hoped she didn't prefer Kodan over me because he was a sigma.

I couldn't believe I was one of the lucky ones to marry her. It was a dream to see her when she went into heat and for me to cuddle her every night.

After the kiss finally ended, I took two steps toward her. She looked at me, a small smile teasing her lips.

"Hi, bodyguard," she joked. "Looks like we're married now."

I could tell she was nervous, and so was I. But I smiled widely to put her at ease.

"May I kiss you?"

She nodded, and I grasped her hands in mine. Her small hands were cold as I squeezed them to comfort her. I cupped the right side of her face as I kissed her on her pink lips. Her lips were soft and pliant under mine. I heard her softly moan over all the clapping of the guests around us. It felt so natural kissing her. Being with her. The kiss exceeded everything I dreamt about as I inhaled her fresh peach scent.

When we broke the kiss, her eyelashes fluttered open, and she gave me a glittering smile. It looked like she didn't think it was awkward marrying me after all.

"It's official now," she said. "My husband."

"And you're my wife."

Voss

IT WAS my turn to kiss the omega bride.

This wasn't a good idea at all. Kodan was being too impulsive.

Once we're married into the Royal Pack, they could turn on us anytime. This was a fucking bad idea. Any infraction on our part could get the entire kingdom to rain down on us. Omegas were greedy for cocks, and if she knew how much bigger a sigma's knot became–she would get scared. I couldn't wait to see her innocent blue eyes widen in shock when Kodan pounded into her.

She was looking at me expectantly.

Fuck.

Flashing my panty-dropping smile, I saw her breasts heaving with desire. I came here every year for the Omega Ball to snag a new omega each time. She was no different. We kissed, and I smelled her peach scent increasing under my spell. She was naïve and innocent. The perfect omega.

"You're perfect," I said against her lips as I pulled away. Her face was pink and flushed. Tendrils of blond hair framed her face as I brushed them away. "You already make a good wife."

"Oh, thanks," she giggled.

All omegas were the same.

∼

Lyra

"CONGRATULATIONS," said Beth half-heartedly as I prepared to say goodbye to everyone. We didn't have a wedding reception, considering how gloomy the occasion was. We were outside the palace, under the full moon, with my family and other royals. I knew my friend felt terrible, but it was nothing like how Yasmeen felt. Yasmeen had literal streaks of mascara running down her cheeks as she hugged me.

"Thank you for saving my life," she sniffed. "You didn't have to marry the brute."

"I wasn't going to let you die," I said, rubbing her back in comfort.

She pulled away, and I smiled to show her I was going to be okay.

"They better treat you good," she said.

"I'll let you know if they don't," I said reassuringly. I turned to my mom and fathers, who were waiting behind Yasmeen and Beth. Walking towards them in my long dress, I hugged them all one by one. My mom fixed the veil behind my head, droplets of tears streaming down her face. "Mama, don't cry."

"I'm trying not to," she said, smiling despite her tears. My eyes burned with unshed tears.

"You're going to make me cry again," I said. "It was completely my choice."

"It's just hard to let my only baby go," she said, full tears running down her face. I remembered the day she lost her second baby and how hard she took it. But it was inevitable that one day, I'd have to leave her. I knew she was lonely in that big palace with her cheating husbands, and my heart ached as I gave her one last hug.

"Everything will be okay, Mama."

After saying goodbye to my fathers, I felt Kodan grab my hand, and Luke grasp my other hand, leading me toward a large truck with a pickup bed. I was instantly confused. Where was I going to sit?

Unsurprisingly, Kodan placed a step stool on the back.

"Are we really going to ride in the back?" I asked. I didn't care if I sounded stuck-up. This was unacceptable.

"I don't have all the riches in the world like your family," said Kodan, ordering one of the Wild Wolfmen to toss my ten suitcases into the truck. I flinched as I saw my suitcases piled on top of each other willy-nilly. I had precious clothes and makeup collections in them.

"I don't want to go in there," I said in a low voice to Kodan.

"Oh yes, you are," he growled, lifting me high and onto the truck.

It was humiliating, but I smiled and waved at everyone as I stood there on the pickup bed like nothing was wrong.

Me, the princess of Howl's Edge, on the back of a damn truck for her wedding day. I wanted to die. I never dreamt of a wedding like this. Kodan was a brute and wasn't even dressed correctly; Voss was a handsome player, and things felt a little awkward between myself and Luke.

I had no idea how any of this was going to work.

Five

KODAN

"You can sit here," I said to the princess, gesturing to my lap. She looked at me with annoyance in her eyes. "You're going to fall if you don't."

She slowly made her way over to me, and I quickly scooped her onto my lap. I deliberately placed her warm ass right over my hard cock. I nearly groaned out loud in the pleasure of her soft ass squirming against me. It had been a while since I last held a female like this. I sniffed in her amazing peach scent, absorbing all her softness.

Luke looked at me warily as he settled down on a large barrel, holding the side of the pickup bed for balance.

"Should I start driving?" Voss called from the front driver's side.

"Yeah, we're good," I said.

The princess was staring straight ahead as we drove past the palm trees and sand of the city. The warm night air caused her white veil to swish around, covering her face nearly entirely. I couldn't see her face or guess what she was thinking. Or if she even felt my hardness between her ass cheeks.

"Where are we going?" she asked without looking at me.

"To my tower," I replied.

"How far away is it?"

"We'll be there in a couple of hours," I said. "Why do you have so many suitcases?"

"My entire life is in those suitcases. I'm not happy how your men just threw it in," she said.

Oh. *That's why she was pouting.*

"Well, it's too late now," I said. "No need to throw a tantrum."

"I'm not throwing a tantrum," she huffed. "An apology for one would help."

Was this princess giving me orders?

"Let me tell you something, princess," I said in a low voice in her ear. I wrapped my arm around her waist, pulling her in closer, squeezing her onto my cock. "I don't take well at being ordered around."

Her breathing deepened, and I could see the side of her face flush pink.

"I can tell," she said, not backing down at all.

Okay, so she wanted to play.

"Do you feel that underneath your ass? The hard stick?"

The color on her face deepened to my satisfaction. The truck shook, going over some gravel, and her bottom bounced on my cock, causing it to harden some more and get even bigger.

I was starting to like this little princess.

"Can I sit somewhere else?" she asked, squirming as I felt her scent getting stronger with arousal.

"Oh no, you're sitting right here, little princess," I said, positioning her directly over my cock again.

"Why don't you just let me go and leave my people alone?"

I pressed my hand against her waist, the soft fabric of her dress between my fingers as I held her tighter.

"It's not happening," I said. "You're my wife now, and you better start acting like it."

The truth was, I wanted my people to stop getting attacked viciously by the secret militia of the Royal Pack. She had no idea what was going on outside of the palace walls besides playing with makeup all day.

"I want to sit with Luke," she said stubbornly.

I laughed softly. She was a brat, but she turned me on in such a way she couldn't imagine.

"I'm the pack leader, and I decide what's happening to you," I said. "For now, you will sit here on my lap until the end of the trip. Unless you want my cock inside of you right now?"

"No," she burst out. And she kept quiet after that. My face cracked into a wide smile.

After a few minutes, I felt her head press against my chest as she slept. Her body was relaxed and pliant against mine in her sleep. My hand inched up her waist. I was dying to cup her ripe, perky breast. It was so soft and so juicy.

I couldn't help but squeeze it tight, and she gasped, waking up.

"It's just me," I said.

"I know it's you. Who else could it be?" she asked sarcastically.

I smelled her scent of desire wafting to my nose.

"Do you like it when I touch you?"

"I'd rather be wide awake for it," she said, jabbing me with her words.

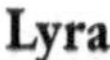

Lyra

I CLOSED my eyes to try sleeping again.

Kodan startled me when he grabbed me like that, but in

truth, my panties were sopping wet. His touch sent shock waves through my body, showing me things I'd never felt before. His entire body enveloping me while I was on his lap was too much. I could feel his strong sigma energy radiating to me and down between my legs. Even though I'd taken my heat suppressant, I was worried it wouldn't work against this sigma.

I had never gone into heat before, and I was terrified of it. When an omega went into heat, they could only think about getting rutted and knotted constantly.

I was learning that Kodan was a sigma that I couldn't mess around with. He knew what he wanted and took what he wanted.

As I tried to sleep, I couldn't help but focus on his rough hands pawing me and his stone penis pressing against my bottom.

Even though I disliked him, my omega body had a mind of its own. My body wanted him inside of me as soon as possible. To quench the ache deep inside.

Luke leaned against the side of the pickup truck; his back turned toward us. I was going to sleep with three males tonight, and I had never slept with even one before.

At home, I was carefully watched throughout my entire life. I wasn't allowed to date anyone or go to real school with all the other omegas and betas. Instead, I received private lessons at the palace, so my virginity was as intact as could be.

I had no idea if sex was going to be painful or if Kodan was going to take me roughly. He was excited, seeing how his hands hadn't left my chest area. I wished I had talked more about this with my cousin, Yasmeen, who was happily mated to a pack.

I RUBBED the sleep out of my eyes. Today's events and the wedding crashed over me as I remembered everything.

I scrambled to get up, realizing I was still on Kodan's lap.

"No need to panic. We're here," said Kodan.

Realizing the truck had stopped, I disentangled myself from him and stood. I was greeted by a crowd of the half-human, half-wolf people I had seen attacking our city. My heart was in my throat as I backed away in a panic, crashing into Luke. They were barking and drooling at the mouth, their eyes on me.

"What's happening?" I asked Kodan. They were looking at me like I was their next dish.

"They think you're our new omega sacrifice," said Kodan, rubbing his black beard, which was as curly as his hair.

"Am I going to be the new sacrifice? Do you sacrifice omegas? Is that a real thing?" I was panicking out of my mind.

"It's a real thing."

"Are you going to let that happen to me?" I asked.

Luke stood protectively in front of me, brandishing his small gun.

Kodan jumped off the truck's bed, waving at the people with both hands, and they began to quiet down. Voss came around the truck to join Kodan.

"She's mine," yelled Kodan, and the crowd began to boo at him. As I looked at the crowd, I was scared to get out of the truck. They all had long fur running down their arms and legs. Most of them didn't have a stitch of clothing on them. Some of the women had pieces of cloth around their waists, but all of them were bare-breasted.

"Come on down," Voss called to me. He had an excited gleam in his eyes. I bit my lip, looking at them. How were they going to protect me against the massive crowd?

I grabbed Luke's hand instinctively.

"You can do this, Lyra," Luke said.

"What if they kill me?"

"I won't let them," he said. "A lot worse will happen if you stay here."

He was right. I had never met these Wild Wolfmen before, and they were unpredictable. Anything could happen to us.

"Do you have my back, Luke?"

"Always."

"Okay, let's do this," I said, allowing him to lead the way.

Six

LYRA

The mud squelched under my heels as we walked past the Wild Wolfmen in this little area of the island. I felt like I hadn't woken up fully from my nap. Like I was stuck in a never-ending nightmare.

I had never been to this remote piece of land on Howl's Edge.

It looked like the world's end since the people lived right next to mountains and rocks. Observing this little village, I noticed little to no houses. The tiny houses were made of mud or bricks. Some people lived outside in massive tents, and some were literally sleeping under palm trees without any blankets. I saw straw and grass mats lying all over the ground.

I had never seen poverty like this, and my heart was saddened as I watched the little kids running around naked, also covered in fur.

"This is terrible," I whispered to Luke.

He was also staring wide-eyed at everything, and I knew he was just as shocked as I was as we walked along the mountain-side following Kodan. Behind us, the Wild Wolfmen carried my suitcases in a procession. They seemed to understand what

Kodan was saying, but they couldn't speak except for barks, growls, or whistles.

"There's my home, just around the corner," said Kodan, pointing to a large tower made of white stones. It was tall and spiraling with treacherous stairs around the building. As we walked towards it, I clasped Luke's hand tightly. I didn't even want to step foot in it, but I didn't have a choice as I carefully climbed up the steps with Luke holding me from behind to ensure I didn't fall to my death.

Kodan swung the front door open.

When we walked inside, I noticed that the stone tower wasn't furnished at all. The first thing that caught my eye was the bare living room with three white pillows lying against the gray walls. The pillows were stained and worn to death. In the middle was a gray shag rug in front of a bare fireplace. The place was spacious but looked empty and unwelcoming.

"Is this where I'm supposed to live?" I asked.

"It's not like your fancy palace," said Voss. "But yes, this is where you'll be living, Miss Princess."

"I can't live like this," I said. Not allowing Voss to intimidate me. "I'm not living here. Can we stay at a hotel or something?"

"Lyra," my bodyguard whispered to me harshly.

Nope. I wasn't having it.

Kodan turned to me, his eyes on me. My body heated instantly under his gaze.

"This is where you'll be living," he said finally. I scowled. His eyes roamed my chest area, his eyes undressing me. "Let's get that wedding dress off of you."

I clenched my thighs together, fighting against the slick that threatened to drip from between my legs.

He grasped my left forearm. His touch was light and delicate but dangerously foreboding as he led me up a set of stairs.

There were several rooms on the second floor, some of them with the doors open.

"That's my room," said Voss, pointing to a clean and neat room. The bed was carefully made without a speck in sight.

"It's clean," I said, stopping to look. He had a single bed in the corner with a large picture frame above it. It was a blown-up picture of him, holding a pen thoughtfully in his hand. He clearly loved himself. "Nice picture."

Kodan let out a chuckle, and Luke grunted. Voss's eyes lit up, and he smiled widely, believing my sarcastic comment to be genuine.

"Thank you," he said.

"My room is down the hall, the last door on the left. Luke, you can pick any room," said Kodan. He opened the door next to Voss's room. It had an alpha-sized mattress on the ground. Cobwebs covered the windows, and the closet was empty. There weren't any curtains, dressers, or mirrors that I had back in the palace. It was a stark contrast to my lavish life at the palace.

And I didn't like it one bit.

A couple of Wild Wolfmen began stacking my suitcases into the room. I swallowed as I watched them. In hindsight, I should've brought a mirror or furniture of my own from the palace.

"We need to go into the city to buy a mirror," I said when the Wild Wolfmen left. Kodan chuckled, ignoring me as he brushed the spiders off the bed.

"Has anyone been in this room before?" asked Luke, also looking around in bewilderment.

"No," said Kodan. "This room was prepared for a potential future shared mate for the pack."

I let go of Luke's hand and walked to my suitcases.

"I want to grab a few things," I said. I really needed my toothbrush, comb, and essentials.

"I'll give you ten minutes," said Kodan, his gaze dark. "Then that dress is coming off."

THE TILE FLOORS of the bathroom felt cold under my feet.

I was slowly brushing my teeth as I looked into the tiny mirror above. My makeup was still on, but my eyeliner was messed up from sleeping on Kodan's lap. Swirls of nervousness and anticipation wracked my belly as I rinsed my mouth.

I was going to sleep with a sigma and two alphas. I was no longer going to be a virgin after tonight.

Every night I'd dream of how my first time would go, and this wasn't how I imagined it would happen.

Not even close.

I was more than willing to lose my V-card, but I wasn't sure about Kodan and Voss. Removing my hairpins next, my heart flipped in excitement, thinking about Luke and how we were married without warning. He was much older than me, but he cared about me. In time, maybe I'd learn to love him. It was easier with Luke.

Kodan was rough around the edges. No softness to him. And Voss was all about himself.

My blond hair lie around my shoulders in large curls. I needed to get back into the room, because my feet were starting to get cold on the bare rug-less stone floor. To my horror, I noticed a large spider with long legs crawling over the mirror.

"Spider!" I screamed, backing away from the mirror and crashing into the wall.

The bathroom door burst open, and Kodan stood at the door, huffing, his face red.

"Where is it?"

"On the mirror, right there," I said, pointing to it and

contorting my body away from it. I couldn't run out of the door since his large body enveloped the tiny bathroom, blocking my way. He brought his hand up to it and smashed it. I looked away, covering my mouth with my hands.

"He's dead," said Kodan, washing his hands in the sink.

I tried to control my erratic breathing when he turned to the towel rack behind me. He reached around my waist, drying his hands on the towel. His body was close up against mine, and my inner wolf nearly swooned at the close contact. It was like my omega knew it was happening. All reason was out the door. I was going to lose my virginity very soon. His hot breath brushed my shoulder as he dried his hands.

"Are you ready for me, princess?" he whispered.

"Yes," I said in a low voice. I wanted to get this over with. To get my horniness out of my system.

He placed his hand on my lower back, pressing me against him. He was hard, and he was ready. His long, dark hair covered my face as he kissed me on the lips. I ground my hips against him as I pressed my lips against his, biting his lower lip.

"Hmm," he said, his eyes slightly widening in surprise. "My princess wants it now. Let's go into the room. Your body-guard is getting impatient."

~

Kodan

I SMELT her eager peach scent as I impatiently unbuttoned the back of her dress.

The white buttons were tiny, slipping through my fingers. My cock was hard and impatient as I tried to go faster. Both alphas' scents were strong as they helped me unbutton this ridiculous dress.

"You're all struggling," said Lyra with a hint of amusement. "My mom buttoned them up in just a couple of minutes."

"Should I just rip it open?" I suggested.

She shook her head frantically. "This was my mother's dress."

"Fuck the dress," I growled, tempted to rip that delicate white cloth apart to expose the rest of her back and bottom.

But I didn't.

Some part of me didn't want to see my omega in tears on her wedding night. The only tears I wanted to see was when I broke her virginity. It was well-known that the princess of Howl's Edge wasn't allowed to be with any alpha except after marriage. She was pure and untouched, unlike the Wild females I had taken. Feral rutting in the village often happened between the people. No thought or jealousy occurred between everyone. No rules at all existed when it came to sex. But I had to be different with Princess Lyra. Holding back my inner feral sigma was difficult in this situation.

Giving up on the buttons, I picked her up and dropped her on the bed, laying her on her back. She yelped in surprise when I lifted her dress over her legs.

"Much easier," said Voss.

"We'll worry about the damn dress later," I growled, gazing at her pale legs covered in stockings. Her thigh had a round white lace cloth tied to it.

"You have to remove the garter with your teeth," she said in a low voice.

"That thing?" I said, touching the cloth.

"It's tradition," she said.

I lowered my face to her thigh, drinking in her delicious scent, which clouded my senses. Grabbing ahold of her thigh with my hand, I tore through the garter with my teeth, ripping it to shreds.

"Is that good?"

"Um, yes," she said sheepishly, her face pink. Her dress ruffled in waves, cocooning her in a sea of creamy white fabric. She was a vision. The little princess looked delectable, her thighs pressed close together in her shyness.

It was time to copulate and make this bride mine.

"I will take her first," I said, all the blood rushing down to my hard cock.

Seven

LYRA

I couldn't believe Kodan ripped the garter to shreds.

His wide body hovered over me, and I couldn't look him in the eyes. I didn't think I'd clam up so fast like this. Kodan tried to separate my legs apart with his knee, but I kept my thighs shut tight together.

My legs were shaking, and I had no idea why.

"What are you doing?" he said.

"I...I can't," I said, tears flooding my eyes instantly. I wanted my wedding night to be about love and not just quick, rough sex.

To my shock, he pulled away, sitting on the edge of the bed. I sat up and pulled my dress down to cover my legs.

"Your job as a wife is to serve her husband," he said. "But I'm not going to take you by force."

"You're not?"

"No," he said, looking at the door and away from me. "Do you feel comfortable if Luke takes you first?"

My heart instantly lifted as I looked at Luke. Luke gave me a small wink.

"I can try," I said.

"Alright," said Kodan, leaving the room without another glance at me. "Are you coming, Voss?"

"No, I'd like to watch," said Voss, the creep.

Oh no, was Kodan furious with me?

I began contemplating all kinds of thoughts, but Luke soon dispelled them by hugging me against his chest. He began purring against me, and I started to feel calmer, feeling his vibrations flow through my body.

My breathing slowed, and my tears stopped. An alpha's purr or growl always did the trick for an omega like me. It was nature's way of calming down an omega, especially when she was in heat and hormones were all over the place.

Luke rubbed my tears away with the back of his thumb, and I sniffed.

"Sorry, I know I'm a weirdo. I chose to get married," I said.

"There's nothing to be sorry for," he said. "You are a virgin, and he was being too rough."

"I thought I could handle it."

"Let me untie those buttons for you, sweetie," said Luke, and I turned around, my back facing him.

I lifted the edge of my dress and dried my eyes, sniffling while he took his time unbuttoning the row down my back. I looked towards the window, lost in the night sky. The moon shone brightly on this side of the island. It wasn't quite a full moon yet.

I noticed that Voss had shed his pants, watching us as he sat on a chair, his hand clutching his penis. It was normal for an omega to be shared by her pack, and I expected this.

But this was my first time.

When Luke finished unbuttoning my dress, I shrugged it off my shoulders, and he helped me get the darn thing off my body. I only wore a white lace bra and a white thong that I saved for my wedding night.

I shyly tried to cover myself, but he grasped my wrists gently, pulling my hands apart.

"So beautiful," he breathed, staring at my body.

He started kissing my wrists and up my arms. His kisses were sensual and slow, burning through my skin. When he reached my shoulder, he brushed my hair to the side, kissing all the way up to my bare neck. I dropped my head to one side, mewling as he kissed me on my collarbone.

Oh, it felt so good when he kissed me there.

His warm lips covered the side of my neck, his teeth grazing my skin. Fire burned in my core, heating through my body. I laid back, pulling him down over me as he continued to kiss my neck. He reached my lips, pressing his mouth hard against mine.

It wasn't like the chaste kiss at the wedding. This was a real kiss.

I moaned against his lips and wrapped my legs around his waist. Luke took his time kissing my neck. Then he flipped my bra down, his mouth finding my aching boobs.

"I want you," I whispered.

Luke

KISSING the princess's breasts didn't feel real to me.

When her parents chose me to become her bodyguard, I never thought I would have feelings for her. I just wanted to do my job and go home. But over the years, she would tell me things. Her dark secrets, her crushes that never amounted to anything. When she turned nineteen, her body matured, and her dresses clung tighter to her body. I tried to shut down my feelings. I was too old for her.

But when she proposed to marry me. My cock had been hard ever since.

Her swollen pink mouth was pouty, the heat between her legs obvious as she rubbed her pussy against me. Her legs wrapped tighter around my waist.

"Shh, sweetie," I replied to her demand, her breast in my mouth. Her breasts were medium-sized, like a ripe mango, turning pink. I suckled her nipples, and she arched her waist to mine. My cock pressed against her, threatening to rip through my pants.

Reaching down, I felt for her center, and my hand came in contact with her wet panties. I squeezed her pussy lightly over her panties, and I felt her slick, dampening her panties even more.

"I'm sorry," she said, her face pink and flushed. Her blond hair was wild around her head.

"Why is your little pussy wet?" I said, teasing her pussy some more, massaging her vulva in circles with my thumb.

"I need you."

"What do you need, exactly?" I shifted her panties to one side and touched her naked pussy. Her flesh was tender and trembling under my fingers. My penis was getting impatient, my alpha wolf wanting to be inside her. She shyly lifted her hand, going inside my dress shirt, slowly feeling my chest.

But I had to take it slowly with her.

She was a virgin. And I knew that for sure. There were countless times when I'd heard her masturbate while I guarded her door at night in the palace. I would remember her nightly moans as I jacked off every night.

"I need your knot," she said softly. Her round eyes widened at her words, and her full lips hesitated to talk dirty.

"What do you want it to do to you?" I pressed, rubbing her swollen clitoris next with the pad of my calloused thumb. "Do you want me inside your tight little pussy?"

"Yes," she gasped when I squeezed her again. She was ready and dripping for me.

Lyra

I PRETENDED Voss wasn't in the room as I pulled my panties off, and Luke quickly removed his pants.

I wanted Luke like never before. Fantasies of him bucking inside me dominated my dreams at night. I was forbidden to sleep with a bodyguard, so I would fantasize about it when I was horny.

Luke settled on top of me again, and my eyes widened at the rod that hung between his legs.

"Can I touch it first?" I asked. I didn't wait for his reply as I wrapped my fingers around it. It was thick and veined. The skin was soft and velvet-like, lengthening as I touched it. It was pulsating when I squeezed.

"Oh, Princess, you're torturing me," he groaned, closing his eyes. "Spread your legs."

After getting acquainted with his penis, I opened my legs for him, and he rubbed his stiff member against my opening, coating it in my slick. I moaned, my stomach clenching with need as he rubbed me frantically.

His alpha cock was touching me but not going inside. I mewled in desperation, and he noticed that, holding my face in both of his hands as he plunged inside of me. Lightening-hot pain speared inside of me, and I nearly screamed.

But the pain slowly dissipated once he broke past my barrier.

He didn't move. He let his cock settle there.

"How's the pain?" he asked, concern etched on his face.

"It's okay," I gasped, not wanting him to stop. "I didn't think my first time would be so painful. It's not like how I imagined it."

"You're so fucking tight," he said. "I don't want to hurt you. Tell me to stop if it hurts."

"Keep going," I said. Once we got past that initial hurdle, it started to feel good as he pulled his cock in and out of me. His penis was like a foreign object inside of me, thrusting aggressively, taking me. Owning me.

"Mate," he growled in my ear, gazing into my eyes with glowing orange eyes in the moonlight.

I almost came apart at his words, shuddering underneath his muscular body, pounding into mine. I caught sight of Voss gripping his own pale cock in his hand, watching me. Slick shot out from me, and I screamed as I finally orgasmed.

"Oh, yes," said Voss creepily, his eyes rolling in the back of his head as he exploded simultaneously.

Luke bucked his hips, his cock going deeper inside of me as he groaned with his own climax. Spurts of his hot liquid filled me.

"Mate," I whispered to Luke as he collapsed on top of me. I felt his cock swelling at the base, stretching my pussy as I hugged him. It felt weird but oddly comforting at the same time. I liked cuddling like this after sex. "How long does the knot usually last?"

"Like twenty minutes," he said.

When I looked back at where Voss was sitting, he was gone.

"Where did they go?" I said, confused. Wasn't I supposed to be mated to all of them?

"Who cares? You have me," said Luke, kissing my temple.

I yawned. I felt warm and safe under Luke.

"Even though my wedding night didn't go as expected–you made it special," I said.

"I'm glad, Lyra," he muttered, kissing me on the lips again.

But the moment was over when Kodan stepped back into the room.

The pack leader stood over us, his eyes flashing briefly upon seeing that Luke was still inside me. Our naked bodies were still entwined around each other, and there was no way I was going to be pulled away from him.

"I see you've broken her virginity," Kodan addressed Luke.

"Yes, I have," said Luke. "At your orders."

"That is true," said Kodan. Then Kodan turned to me. "You will spend the entire day with me tomorrow. We will get to know each other better. Then tomorrow night will be your true wedding night."

Eight

LYRA

"I think getting to know each other better sounds nice," I said in agreement, without thinking what would happen tomorrow night with him.

At least we had more time.

Kodan looked satisfied that I'd complied with his new plan. I didn't mind getting to know him. With the scar over his eye, ripped-up shirt, and muscles bulging out of his arms, he was intimidating and made this large room feel so small.

My pussy clenched tight around Luke's cock, which was slowly receding in size.

"I want Luke with me, though," I said, my voice low with uncertainty.

"That's fine," said Kodan. "But tonight, I'll be sleeping next to you."

I was locked in place by Luke's knot while Kodan settled next to me, sinking the bed further on the ground.

I couldn't run away as his body came close to mine, my back facing him. He wasn't touching me, but I could feel the heat emanating from his body- calling to me.

Warmth flooded my privates, and Luke gave me a knowing look. He knew the effect this sigma was having on my body.

My face heated with embarrassment.

"Where's Voss?" I asked, trying to break the awkward silence.

"He likes sleeping in his room," explained Kodan. "You will spend time with him later this week."

Luke's knot finally released me, but I stayed facing him with my back still to Kodan. Kodan draped the gray mothball-smelling sheet over my naked body when I yawned again.

Luke kissed me on the lips again as I closed my eyes.

"Sleep tight, my princess."

Sometime in the middle of the night, I didn't realize I had turned on my back.

I groggily noticed Kodan's hand was on my thigh, and he was snoring. But when I moved, his hand ventured up and grasped my vagina. Oh, my goodness. I didn't want to cause a scene and cause us both to be embarrassed, so I didn't move a muscle.

But the longer he held me between my legs, the more I felt the warmth gathering in my core again.

I was getting horny from his touch even though he was sleeping.

His hand twitched, and his middle finger slipped between the folds of my pussy. I bit my lip to keep from slicking all over his hand. His finger stayed inside me for a good minute while I debated whether to move his hand. Slick began to moisten my pussy as I tried to think of a way to move him without waking him and facing him.

His thick sausage finger began to thrust inside me.

I held my breath.

Kodan had stopped snoring, but his eyes were still closed. I covered my mouth with my fist as he fingered me while Luke slept soundly on my other side. Then he inserted a second finger, and I let my legs fall open, making it easier for his second finger to go inside me, stretching me out. I knew his fingers were probably drenched, but I didn't care at this moment.

I was teetering on the edge now. Heat spiked through my tummy and down my core.

"Do you want a third finger?" Kodan rasped in my ear. I jumped, my face heating immediately as I clenched my thighs together.

He was fucking awake this whole time. *How long had he been awake?*

I shook my head, a bout of shyness overtaking me. I grasped his giant hand, trying to pry him away. But he kept his fingers firmly inside me.

"No third finger," I whispered, hoping against hope that Luke wouldn't wake up. It was humiliating that I was enjoying the sigma's touch.

"Does this feel good?" he asked, hooking his fingers upward and touching my g-spot.

Slick coated me between my legs in response. I needed relief. I needed him to finish the job so badly. He turned on his side, staring at me with those golden eyes of his.

"Please."

"Open your legs," he commanded in his sigma baritone, compelling me to obey. It was more powerful than an alpha's command. And in my sleepy state of mind, I was powerless against him.

My legs fell open again of its own accord, falling prey to his command. At the same time, I was excited, but I didn't want him to know that.

"Okay."

"I'm going to ask again. Do you want me to stick a third finger inside your tight little pussy?"

The thought was appealing. My pussy was clenching around his fingers like a lifeline.

"Yes," I gasped out.

When he plunged the third finger inside me, I cried out.

"Do you like this?" he asked as he began to thrust all three fingers in and out of me. Over and over. Spreading me as wide as possible. I was no longer a virgin. But I still felt like one, even having someone else's fingers inside me.

I nodded to avoid waking Luke, and Kodan plunged his fingers deeper inside. I fisted my hand in my mouth, muffling a scream as my body convulsed with one powerful orgasm.

When I finished, Kodan removed his fingers and shut his eyes—snoring and falling back into a deep sleep.

I quietly yawned, stretching like a cat, and closed my eyes with a smile on my lips.

"PRINCESS, IS SOMETHING WRONG?" Luke asked me the next morning.

I was rifling through my suitcase this morning, looking for my heat suppressants. I was irritated and grouchy for no reason at all.

I didn't feel like talking to Luke right now. Was Luke like the others, just waiting to knot me?

Was he even a genuine friend? I couldn't decide whether to trust him.

"No, Luke," I sighed. "I'm just trying to find something to wear for my date today with Kodan."

"And me," Luke reminded me. "I'm coming with you, remember?"

"First of all, it was my idea to marry you. So don't act like you were the one who wanted to guard me."

"I do want to guard you. That is my job," said Luke.

"So I'm just a job to you?" I snapped.

"I'll meet you downstairs," said Luke, his jaw twitching. "Maybe by then, you'd have control over your emotions because I have no idea what's gotten into you."

I waited until I heard his footsteps squeak down the wooden stairs, and then I collapsed on top of my suitcase, groaning aloud.

I was wearing a fluffy pink bathrobe after my shower. The tub was horrible, with secret spiders in every corner.

If I was going to live in this abandoned tower, I'd have to start making it a little more comfortable and deep-clean everything. It might've contributed to my bad mood this morning.

The smell of fried eggs wafted into the room. I hadn't seen Voss or Kodan this morning yet, and I was definitely nervous to see Kodan again.

Especially after last night's events.

Maybe Kodan was smug and proud of himself. I had no idea. I hated feeling like this. Being an omega was hard when all males saw me only as a sexual object.

I couldn't trust anyone.

I felt more alone than anything, even if Luke was here. But here he was, angry at me, and it was all my fault.

IT WAS sunny outside for a November day.

I was walking alongside Kodan amongst the villagers, with Luke following close behind.

Luke and I hadn't exchanged a word since our spat this morning.

Adjusting my tiara, which had become tangled in my hair, I was aware of the Wild Wolfmen staring at me. I suddenly regretted wearing my royal purple dress, which looked outlandish compared to their minimal to bare clothing.

As we walked, Kodan pointed out the various landmarks, people, and buildings. To me, everything looked rundown, and the people looked frightening with the fur on their bodies along with their fangs sticking out of their mouths.

I wanted to be anywhere but here.

"Look, that's the mango man," said Kodan, pointing out to the man squatting on the ground and mashing mangos in a brown clay pot. He looked up at us with a large, fanged smile.

I was aware of Luke just behind me, looking to see what was happening. I didn't turn to look at him, but I felt his alpha scent come nearer to me.

"Is he making juice out of it?" asked Luke.

"I want two cups," requested Kodan from the mango man.

To my dismay, Kodan forced me to take a cup, and I stared at the gloopy mess in the tin cup.

The mango man barked at me, which I took as a sign to drink it up. I swallowed nervously and brought the cup to my lips, taking a small sip. It was really sweet, not like the mangoes in the city. I chewed the pulp awkwardly and smiled at the mango man with a thumbs up.

"It's good," I said, handing Kodan the tin cup. "But I'm full from the wonderful breakfast you made. Do you want the rest?"

Kodan gruffly took the cup and downed it in one go, handing the mango man the empty cup along with some spare change. Luke had already finished his cup and was somehow making conversation with the mango man.

Luke seemed to be adapting to this place faster than I was. The mango man wasn't even saying real words, just barking and howling, talking with his hands.

"They can't talk?" I whispered to Kodan.

"They can understand us but are unable to speak," replied Kodan gruffly, with a faraway look in his eyes.

"Oh," I said, looking at the mango man in pity.

But the pity for the people soon dispersed. I felt someone grab my hair, and my head yanked back. I screamed as I lost my balance and fell backward.

"Let go of her!" shouted Luke, pointing his gun at the person holding me against him. Barks and whistles sounded. I instantly knew it was one of the Wild Wolfmen.

"Ew, oh my god," I screamed. "Get him off me!"

Kodan barked in another language, and they released my hair.

I got up from the muddy ground, grabbing Luke's hand. My scalp burned as I massaged my head. I turned to see who the hell had grabbed me and saw a Wild Wolfman with a leer on his face and saliva dripping from his chin. He was panting and staring at me with wide, yellow eyes.

"I can't live here!" I shouted at Kodan.

Nine

KODAN

amn it to hell.

The villagers were getting restless. And I had to calm down my very frantic omega wife.

"Shh," I said, pulling her reluctant body to me in a hug. Her body was stiff as I hugged and purred against her. She slowly relaxed under my lead, letting her head fall against my chest. Her tiara dug into my chest as I petted her hair. Her scent filled my senses as I breathed in deeply.

"Just because you can calm me like that doesn't mean I'm not angry," she said, trying to resist my purr.

"It doesn't matter if you're angry. This is your home now," I commanded.

Princess Lyra pulled away from me and punched me in the chest. My eyes widened in surprise. I hadn't seen her this upset before.

"Every villager wants me dead," she exclaimed. "What kind of life is that?"

Then she turned to Luke, and I could see the tension between them. *What happened between them?* He was the lucky bastard to take her virginity last night.

"Are you two fighting?" I asked, shaking my head.

I realized we were still standing next to the mango seller, who was staring at us curiously. I grabbed Lyra's hand to keep walking so I could show her something.

"She doesn't trust me," explained Luke, following close behind.

"I *do* trust you," said Lyra, unconsciously squeezing my hand from her nervousness. "Thank you for saving me, Luke."

"You're welcome," he said in a stiff voice.

"Where are we going now?" Lyra asked me, looking at the mountain next to us.

"I want to show you something. Something that could help you understand," I said.

"Understand what?" she said, looking at me with wide blue eyes. "There's nothing to understand. Just get me the hell out of here."

I led them to a wide clearing of rocks. In front of us was a path of stones over the ocean, like a bridge that led to a cave. A long, screeching howl came from the dark cave.

Lyra stood frozen, staring at the cave.

"I wanted to show you that," I said.

"What the fuck was that? What's in that cave?" she asked, backing away from the stone bridge.

"That is the Shadow Wolf," I explained. I debated whether to tell her the whole story.

"What's that?" asked Luke, one foot on the bridge, trying to get a look into the cave.

"He used to be a sigma, like me," I explained. "Before the Wild Wolfmen and before this village formed."

"So what happened?" Lyra asked, sensing my hesitance.

"Do you remember the Great Moon Revolt? You might've been too young to remember," I said. "He was obsessed with the Royal Pack and wanted more for the less fortunate. He led a revolt against the palace, but he never made it there."

"What do you mean?" said Luke. "I've heard about revolts happening here and there."

"A witch cursed him and his people," I explained. "Zaneesha cursed him until he became a wild wolf beast, who we call the Shadow Wolf. He began to attack his own followers, who were also transformed into Wild Wolfmen."

"That's hard to believe," said Lyra, looking at me with pity. "Do you actually believe this stuff?"

"I saw it with my own eyes," I said. "Before the Shadow Wolf could kill off the rest of his people, I trapped him in there. In that cave."

"Why didn't you just kill him?" asked Luke.

He was my younger brother. And the only family I had left.

"I couldn't kill a fellow sigma," I said instead.

"So what does this have to do with me?" asked Lyra.

"Every year on the full moon, the villagers present an omega to the Shadow Wolf as an offering to satiate his appetite," I explained.

"Oh," she said, realization dawning on her face.

"Tomorrow is the full moon, but I had told them there would be no more sacrifices after I married you," I said.

"Why did you agree to marry me?"

"I wanted peace for the people," I said. "They were being picked off one by one by the Royal Pack's guards. It was time to change something and they don't understand."

We started to walk away from the sight of the cave and continued down the shoreline of the ocean. Giant rocks blocked our view of the village as we walked. This was a rougher area of the terrain, the waves cracking against the rocks.

～

Lyra

I WASN'T sure whether or not to believe Kodan's story.

It sounded almost like a fairytale, so it was unbelievable to me. I kept glancing over at the ominous cave and the sad howls that emanated from it.

Kodan was serious every time he spoke, which made me believe he wasn't kidding. We were walking down towards the shoreline and behind the giant rocks that separated us from the village.

My foot slipped on a rock, and I yelled when my tiara splashed into the water. Releasing Kodan's hand, I kicked off my heels and ran into the cold water.

"Lyra! Come back," Kodan called, chasing after me.

The tiara was from my mom. I couldn't lose it.

A huge wave crashed over my head, and I spewed out water as I tried to see.

"No, it's gone," I groaned, rubbing the water from my eyes. My purple and gold dress soaked through, dragging behind me as I waded deeper into the water.

"You're not going to find it," said Luke, pulling me out of the water.

Sorrow filled my heart as I stared off into the water, following Luke's lead. I couldn't see the beautiful tiara anywhere. I felt like I had left my family all over again, stuck in this wild wasteland.

The air was cooler below the rocks, and I shivered as a gust of wind shot through.

"I need to take this off," I said. "Can you please help me unzip the dress, Luke?"

It was still tense between us as he came around and helped me take my large dress off. I stood there in my undergarments. My thin white bra and panties were soaked.

Goosebumps rose from my skin as I hung the dress over a boulder.

"You're bleeding," said Kodan, coming up beside me and

touching my right arm. I looked to see a streak of blood running down my elbow from the scratch on my upper arm. I hadn't even felt it when I ran after the tiara. A look of softness came over his eyes. "You're so crazy, little princess."

"That tiara was from my mom years ago. I've had it since I was twelve," I tried to explain.

Kodan ripped off the bottom portion of his shirt, showing off his muscular stomach, as he began to wrap my arm. Luke held me from behind to stop me from running back into the water as Kodan stood in front of me. Sandwiched between them, I felt trapped in the powerful male energies surrounding me. I clenched my thighs when I started to feel the familiar warmth blooming in my middle.

"I'm sorry you lost your tiara," said Kodan.

"You're being strangely nice to me," I said, suspicious and not yet trusting of him. "What happened?"

"I can still be a brute if you like that," said Kodan, narrowing his eyes as he finished wrapping my arm, his fingers lingering on my skin. "You're shivering."

"Yes, just a little," I said, my teeth chattering against my will.

Kodan pressed his hard body against me, and when I tried to pull away, my back pressed against Luke's warm body. I felt something hard press against my back and realized it was Luke's erection.

"Don't worry, we'll warm you up," said Kodan, rubbing his callused hands on my arms. I pressed my cold face against his chest, breathing him in. He smelled like the outdoors, fresh and wild. Luke squeezed the water from my wet hair as I snuggled against Kodan for warmth.

Kodan

My wife needed me.

I enjoyed the feeling when she pressed her cold button nose against my chest. Her small breasts jutted out, nipples pink and hard under the sheer fabric. My cock was growing harder by the minute.

I needed her.

And she was going to fulfill her wifely duties today. When her shivering finally began to cease, I lifted her chin with my finger.

"Feeling better now?" I asked.

"Yes," she said, biting her lower lip as she squinted from the sun.

"What are you thinking about?"

"I'm thinking about tonight and how I want to get it over with," she said.

"What do you mean?"

"I want to do it now."

I laughed, looking at all the rocks around us. "There isn't exactly any comfortable place around here."

She pressed her breasts against me, grinding her hips against my pelvic region. All this cuddling had somehow turned her on. My lips descended onto hers as I breathed her in.

Ten

LYRA

This was impulsive.

But when Kodan's lips captured mine, I stopped regretting my decision.

I wanted him.

After he had opened up today, I felt closer to Kodan. Kodan had opened my eyes to the potential of being with him. I wasn't doing this to save my people anymore. Since I was still pressed up against Luke's body behind me, Luke began kissing my neck.

My clothes were drenched against my skin, but I was heating up quickly in the middle of my new husbands.

"Are you sure you want me to take you right here? Right now?" asked Kodan.

He looked shocked and surprised that I wanted it right then. It gave me a sort of satisfaction to be in charge of this situation and to catch him off guard.

I pulled my bra down, releasing my breasts seductively.

"I'm pretty sure," I said softly. The tent in his pants bulged from his erect penis. The anticipation of waiting until night to have sex with him was driving me crazy.

Luke grasped my breasts while still standing behind me.

"Use me as a cushion," Luke whispered in my ear, and my stomach fluttered with excitement at the thought.

I relaxed against him while he warmed my breasts in his hands, squeezing them. Kodan was kissing my neck, biting softly with his teeth without piercing my skin.

"Can you handle me, little princess?" Kodan asked in his rough voice, biting my earlobe gently while his thick beard tickled my skin.

Warmth fluttered in my belly. My breathing accelerated at his words.

"I...I can handle it," I stuttered, a little intimidated by what this big sigma would do to me. He was huge, and his member hung between his legs.

He cupped my pussy while I stood leaning against Luke.

Suddenly, I felt self-conscious as I looked around to see if anyone was watching. There wasn't anyone around for miles. I guess no one wanted to get close to the Shadow Wolf. The only thing around for miles was the ocean beating against the rocks. I was alone with an alpha and a sigma who desired me.

The thought turned me on even more like nothing else. Then Kodan unexpectedly released my pussy from his hold.

I was taken aback and shocked he would reject me like this. He kissed me soundly on the lips with a smile.

"Not right now," he whispered in my ear, and I shivered. "Put your dress back on. We're going home."

He walked away, standing on a boulder with his eyes on the cave.

"Wow," I said to myself, distancing myself from them. I didn't dare look at Luke either, in case I caught him smirking at me or something. Then, gripping my wet dress, I slowly slid it on, still stung by the rejection.

~

Voss

"CALM DOWN, CALM DOWN!" I shouted.

Our people were upset, barking in my face and waving their arms. I knew what they wanted. They wanted an omega this year for the sacrifice but hadn't gotten it.

Earlier in the day, I had gone into the city to buy a ridiculous mirror for the princess at Kodan's orders. We weren't servants to the Royal Pack anymore. Kodan was getting dangerously too close to the princess. All he needed was pussy, and he could easily knot any of the females here instead.

Plus, they were much more fun in bed. Feral and willing to go into any position.

When I came back into the village after my trip, the Wild Wolfmen had cornered me, and I was clutching the full-body mirror in front of me like a shield.

Every year, I'd bring them an omega, but this time, Kodan banned me from taking one. The Omega Ball was thriving with the valuable omegas we needed, and he actually stopped me.

"Omi, omi," chanted the Wild Wolfmen. They were saying 'omega' for short.

I raised my hand, and when they finally quieted down, I was able to speak.

"Yes, we all know the full moon is tomorrow," I started. "But I didn't come without an omega. So, I will offer our omega. Kodan's omega to the Shadow Wolf."

Cheers resounded throughout the village.

Yes, Kodan would be furious. But in the end, he'd realize that we were in charge and the Royal Pack would be at our mercy.

~

Lyra

THAT SAME NIGHT, we were back in Kodan's tower.

I washed my dress in the bathtub, wearing just my robes and slippers. They didn't have a washer or dryer out here in the wild, which sucked. Also, I never had to wash my own clothes. The beta servants usually took care of that.

The soap was harsh against my skin as I rinsed the dress, the purple dye flowing down into the drain. The men were eating dinner, and I finally had a chance to talk to Voss for a moment as he prepared a nice dish of fancy noodles. He was pleasant but guarded for some reason. I wondered if he would loosen up after my date with him tomorrow.

After I squeezed the dress dry, I looked around for a place to hang it and decided the shower rod would have to do.

Two sharp knocks sounded at the bathroom door. Annoyance flowed through me.

I had ignored Kodan since he rejected me earlier, and I still hadn't talked much to Luke about anything. There was a lot of work to be done still, but I had a tendency to avoid confrontation at all costs. I hated being stressed, and I'd rather just avoid the person entirely.

"Yes?" I called, throwing the dress over the metal rod as it dripped onto the floor.

I opened the door and saw Kodan standing there with determination written all over his face. His thick eyebrows were pulled tightly together, and his mouth was set in a tight expression. His long hair was loose around his bare shoulders, and he only wore a pair of black boxers that were tight on his upper thighs.

I couldn't help but gaze at his bare stomach and the thin trail of dark hair that led down to his privates. His body was buff, chiseled in all the right places.

"Why are you avoiding me?" he asked gruffly, staring at me like I didn't have clothes on.

His eyes zeroed in on my chest, covered in my flimsy robe. He advanced toward me, wrapping his fingers around my forearm under the sleeve of my robe.

"Well, you didn't want me earlier," I said, turning to the sink and washing my hands.

Shit, my hands were all purple from the dye. Grabbing the soap bar, I tried scrubbing it off.

Suddenly, Kodan came up behind me, pinning me against the sink.

"Are you telling me you don't want it now?" he asked, bringing his mouth to my ear, whispering harshly.

He made sure I heard every word. My heart rate intensified, and my breathing became fast and shallow.

"You don't get the right to take me whenever you want," I said in a low voice.

His foot pressed between my legs, separating them, and I grew weak with desire. His beard brushed against my neck, and his mouth on my ear worked in tandem to arouse every inch of me. He wasn't even trying, and I was already a wet mess. My omega body betrayed me with every stroke and every word this sigma breathed in my ear.

He licked my earlobe, nibbling on it.

"You don't get the right to tell me what to do," he growled. "Did you want me to rail you against a rock? My own wife?"

"No...but," I grasped the sink, my arms weak. "We're not even really married."

"What the fuck are you talking about? You're my wife, and I'm your husband."

"It's not like we chose it."

Suddenly, his hand snaked inside my robe, cupping my pussy from behind. This time, I didn't have underwear on as I felt his rough hand palming me and driving me wild with the combination of his teeth nibbling my ear from behind.

Slick gushed from me, and my scent covered the bathroom.

"I chose to marry you," he said adamantly. Then he stuck a finger inside of me, and I moaned. "And you will start acting like my wife."

"You're an uncivilized brute," I burst out.

"Then maybe I'll keep acting like a brute," he growled in anger, sticking a second finger inside me. I tried to hump his fingers, but he had me pinned.

I couldn't move at all.

"Please."

"Please, what?"

"I need release...like how you did last night. With your fingers," I said, trying to say it in a commanding tone. His hard body pressing up against mine made it hard to gain control of this situation.

His sigma energy was too much, and it was dominating.

I couldn't talk to him, like how I did with Luke. I was starting to regret how I treated Luke this morning.

"Apologize then," he ordered.

"For what?" I said.

"For calling me a brute," he said. "You're a spoiled little princess from the Royal Pack, aren't you?"

He stuck a third finger inside of me, and I moaned again as he stretched me. My legs were wide open, and I wanted his fingers to move a little. I needed some friction inside me, and he wasn't giving it to me.

"Fine, I'm sorry," I said at last.

He removed his fingers and lifted my robe over my butt, bending me over the sink.

He rubbed his hand over my ass cheeks, squeezing both in turn. It stung, and then he spanked me under the palm of his wide hand. I yelped as he massaged the sting away.

"I will knot you now," he growled.

Kodan lifted me in his arms, taking me by surprise and carrying me into the bedroom. Then he threw me onto the mattress, and I squealed, landing face down.

The sigma meant business tonight.

Eleven

KODAN

The omega's scent grew stronger with her arousal.

She lay still on her stomach, waiting in anticipation for me to make a move.

To ravish her senseless.

I knew she wanted it when she lifted her cute bottom in the air and arched her back.

My cock hardened as I stared at her waving bottom. I smacked her butt over her robes, and she squealed again.

"That's for attempting to challenge me," I growled.

This little princess wasn't going to challenge me under any circumstances. I had reason not to have sex with her at the ocean today. It was dangerous, and she put herself at risk by weakening me with her arousal.

Taking an omega right in front of the Shadow Wolf's cave was dangerous. Omegas were for him, or he thought they were. Having sex next to the rocks would have been her death if the Shadow Wolf grew enraged enough to come after me in my weakest state.

I lifted her robe, exposing her blushing cheeks once again. Kneeling behind her, I was captivated by her dripping and glistening pussy.

I pressed my face into her sopping-wet pussy, and she gasped. I swiped my tongue over her labia, and her ass jutted out further, grinding into my face.

"I'm sorry," she said, her voice weak with desire.

"That's not enough."

"Then what do I do?"

"Come for me," I ordered, licking her clitoris slowly and sensually. I spread her pussy lips apart, staring into her glistening hole. I stuck my finger once again inside of her.

She was so tight. *So delectable.*

"I can't do it on command," she cried out, trying to squeeze her thighs together, but I held her legs apart.

"Release your slick," I said, sucking on her engorged pink clitoris. "Now."

I flicked my tongue in circles around her clit. Adding more pressure.

At my command, her pussy trembled, and slick seeped out between her shaking thighs to my satisfaction.

"Holy shit," she moaned into the pillow as I licked her slick. I wanted every drop of her peach scent on my tongue.

Lyra

I WAS STILL TREMBLING from my orgasm while he continued to lick every drop of slick that I had released.

I tried to control my rapid breathing, trying to gain control of myself. Never did I think I could orgasm on command like that. I underestimated a sigma's power in his commands. It was forceful, and my body willingly obeyed.

"I'm going to go inside of you now, princess," he said, still on top of me. My pussy was throbbing and ready for him to plunge inside. I was still sore from Luke breaking my virginity, but it had gotten much better.

I was more than ready.

The girth of his penis spread my pussy lips wide as he roughly shoved himself into me.

I bit the pillow, feeling every ridge and every curve of his penis straining to get inside me. His cock was huge. The length of it still tried to ram inside me.

"You're huge," I gasped, biting the pillow. It didn't hurt, but it stretched me out like nothing else, stretching me to my limits.

"Yes, I am," he whispered. "Get ready for this, baby."

Then, the thrusts began.

He pulled out, but not all the way. And then he slammed back into me. His cock was solid and firm inside my pussy. Filling me. My hips moved in rhythm with his during every hard thrust and gasp that emitted from my lips.

I tried to stay quiet. But it was impossible.

"Oh *moons*," I gasped into the pillow when he pressed his hands over mine, pinning me beneath him while jackhammering me from behind.

His cock was relentless in its thrusts.

My pussy was tight around him, pulling him even deeper into me, milking his cock into me. Finally, he exploded inside me, howling out loud. His warm liquid shot in bursts into my womb, and then his cock swelled, blocking the semen from seeping out of me.

But the swelling wasn't stopping, and my eyes widened at the sensation.

"A sigma's knot is double the size of an alpha's knot," he whispered, collapsing behind me and pulling me close.

"My pussy is too small for it," I gasped, feeling his knot getting bigger. "It's stretching me."

"Relax, little princess. If I pull it out now, it'll hurt you, baby," he said, rubbing my belly. "We will create cute pups."

"I'm taking heat suppressants," I said. The heat suppressants also worked as a form of birth control for omegas. He growled his disapproval.

"You are married now," he said. "You're not going to take them anymore."

Once an omega mated into a pack, it was up to the alpha to decide whether she should stay on heat suppressants. He had a right to have babies if he wanted.

"I can't."

"Why?"

"I don't trust you," I said. "This marriage was a ploy to stop you from eviscerating my people. So what reason should I have to stop my heat suppressants?"

"Damn," he said. His hand stopped on my belly button, no longer affectionately rubbing me. "We're starting to have a connection."

"It's lust talking," I said.

I knew it was mean, but I refused to trust the warm feelings that arose within me when he cuddled me. I liked it and didn't want it to stop. As we waited for his knot to deflate, it was pretty awkward laying there in silence.

"It's not just lust," he said. "I think I'm starting to...I don't know. Maybe you're right."

Was he about to admit his feelings for me? That I was his one true mate?

Right then, I wasn't sure either, but the warm fuzzy feelings kept growing inside my heart, and I could feel it in my chest. It was crazy because we had known each other for less than two days.

〜

WALKING downstairs in the cold stone tower, I cinched my robe tighter around me. Kodan had fallen asleep while his knot rested inside of me.

I caught sight of Luke sitting on the floor of the empty living room, reading an old newspaper that he must have found on the wooden bookshelf.

I quietly snuck away, wondering where Luke was. I knew he was still upset with me, but I had to make things right.

"Hey, Luke," I greeted, stepping down the last step.

He turned and looked up at me warily.

"Are we on speaking terms now?" asked Luke, setting the newspaper down. The dust from the paper settled around in little particles in the air.

I sat next to him on the floor, pulling my knees up to my chest, and leaned against the cold wall. Luke quickly grabbed one of the pillows, shoving it behind my back so I didn't get cold. My heart warmed at his caring gesture, and I suddenly felt bad.

"I was scared," I began. "I wasn't sure if you really cared for me or if you were just waiting for an opportunity to marry me. Alphas will always hunt omegas."

"I care for you, Lyra," he said without hesitation, and I believed him. "I know how you feel about alphas in general. But I swear to you that even if you don't want to be with me, I still want to stay friends with you."

"Are you serious?"

"Dead serious."

"I believe you," I sighed, leaning against his arm. He wrapped his other arm around me, pulling me in for a hug. He purred, a deep rumble from his chest vibrating into my body, calming my racing heart.

"I miss you," he said. "I miss the fun we used to have. The constant talking."

"You mean *my* constant talking," I laughed, willing to admit that.

"How are you feeling, though? With the sigma?"

"Do you mean Kodan?" I said, winking at him. I wondered if they would ever become close friends or even acquaintances.

"Yes, are you okay with everything?"

"For now, I think I'll be fine," I said. I wasn't trusting of my own feelings yet, and I didn't want to talk about it.

"Are the feelings fluttering inside you?"

"It is," I giggled. It was a running joke between us whenever I spotted an attractive alpha when Luke escorted me somewhere. "But I don't know whether to trust him."

"He hasn't broken his pact yet and hasn't sent his Wild Wolfmen onto the mainland."

"It's only been two days," I said. "He could easily throw me to the wolves. Literally."

"If that ever happens, he'll have to answer to me," said Luke, his chest going up and down rapidly with his intense emotions. I could sense how much he cared for me, and I felt at ease with him again.

He was still my best friend, and I hadn't lost that.

"Is it weird we're married?" I asked out of the blue.

"Because I used to be your bodyguard?"

"Yes."

"Not at all," he said, tilting my chin up for a kiss, his sideburns scratching my face.

He pressed his lips to mine, and I kissed him back.

So far, I felt comfortable with Luke being my husband, and my heart fluttered at the mention of Kodan. Voss was absent, and I promised myself I'd make an effort with him tomorrow.

I locked my hands around Luke's neck, breathing in his strong alpha pinewood scent as I melted into his kiss. We were alone in the living room, but I didn't care, even if someone was watching.

They were all my husbands now, and that took getting used to.

Luke's hand went inside my robe, grasping my left breast in his hand. He broke the kiss and lowered his head to suck on my nipple while still grasping my breast.

A stream of arousal gathered in my core again as I arched my back, offering him my breasts. I had to meet the needs of every male in my pack. Omegas were rare, so we were shared with a pack. It was a fact of life on the island. Omegas were needed to produce strong babies.

As I sat on his lap, my bathrobe opened to expose my naked, shaved pussy.

I wrapped my legs around his waist, grinding against his hips. Luke quickly shed his black shirt and unzipped his pants, his cock springing free from its constraint. I grasped it, feeling the length of it, squeezing the shaft. He groaned and pushed my breasts together, sucking on both my nipples at the same time.

His finger found my pussy.

"You're soaked," he said. I began grinding on his finger, and he chuckled. "Let me give you something bigger."

Twelve

LYRA

T he next morning, I couldn't find my heat suppressant pills anywhere as I dug around my suitcase.

"*No, no, no,*" I said out loud to the empty room. "What did you do, Kodan?"

My clothes were scattered everywhere on the floors. I sat in front of my many suitcases, sighing in defeat, remembering our conversation from last night.

The rain started to pit-patter outside, droplets hitting the bare window, fitting my mood.

Without my heat suppressants, I was vulnerable.

I could go into heat and get pregnant by any one of these males. I've never experienced going into heat, but I've heard it was painful. Fuming, I walked towards the bathroom but stopped when I saw a large, full-body mirror sitting behind the bedroom door. There was a yellow sticky note on it:

I'm out hunting, but have a nice day, my love. Do you like the mirror?- K

The note ended with a picture of a hand-drawn heart. *Oh, wow.* My heart began to soften a little toward Kodan.

I traced the heart with my finger, not realizing I had a smile on my face until Luke walked into the room.

"Well," he said. "What do you have there?"

"Nothing," I said, trying to hide the note by covering it with my hand, but he had already read it over my shoulder.

"The brute actually has feelings," said Luke, kissing my neck while hugging me from behind. I leaned into him, absorbing his alpha strength.

"Of course, he has feelings," I said, turning to kiss Luke on the lips.

"I would draw hearts for you every day if I knew that would make you happy," muttered Luke.

We heard a cough behind us, and we pulled apart, startled by the intruder.

Voss was in the room, staring at us. It felt like I hadn't seen him in forever. His shiny black hair was slicked back, and he wore a nice suit. He smelled strongly of cologne, which covered his natural scent.

"Sorry for interrupting. Hello, my dear," said Voss, grabbing my hand and kissing the top of it.

"Good morning," I greeted. Voss was in a chipper mood, nearly bouncing on his feet. I thought it was cute that he was so excited.

"You should get ready for our big date today," said Voss. I'm looking forward to talking to you one-on-one. Maybe we could leave your burly bodyguard at home?"

"Not a chance. I'm coming," said Luke.

"Are you sure? You'll get bored," said Voss, trying to discourage him.

"I would prefer that Luke comes with us," I said slowly. Voss was finally showing some emotion toward me, and I didn't want to ruin his happy mood.

"Okay, no big deal," said Voss. Then he kissed me on the

cheek. "How about you put something sexy on? We'll pretend your stalker bodyguard isn't there."

I couldn't help but giggle after seeing Luke's face turn red with annoyance.

~

VOSS HELD a large red umbrella over us as we walked through the village.

The rain was on and off.

Today, I wore something a little more practical. Even though I had tons of dresses for my royal gatherings, I was glad I had the presence of mind to pack riding clothes. I wore brown leather leggings, boots, and a white shirt that clung to my chest, topped off with a leather jacket.

My hair was done up in a high bun to combat the rain outside.

Every day, I still wanted to leave this village. But each day, I would see Kodan giving in charity to the Wild Wolfman, and he genuinely cared about them.

He cared about them like they were his own family.

And in a way, I respected that. But I had always dreamt of setting up a beauty salon, but it looked damn near impossible here in the village.

"Luke is following way too close," Voss whispered to me under the umbrella. "I can't even sneak a kiss with you. You're hot as fuck today."

I laughed.

"You can still kiss me," I said. "I promise Luke won't bite."

"It's creepy," said Voss as we stopped in front of a market stall selling knitted blankets.

The older female behind the stall was showing me a large, knitted blue and green blanket. She was topless, with sagging boobs covered in white hair.

"It's cute," I said, taking the knitted blanket from her.

"Let me buy that for you," said Voss.

"It's okay, I brought money," I said, but before I could pull any change out of my leather jacket, Voss had already paid. "Thank you."

As we walked away from the seller, I clutched the cozy blanket to my chest. I couldn't wait to add this to the failing mattress.

"You're welcome," said Voss. "How do you like the mirror I bought for you too?"

"I thought Kodan got it."

"Kodan? Our lazy pack leader made me do all the hard work," said Voss, wiggling his eyebrows animatedly. "He thinks I have time to drive hours into the city to grab a mirror."

I laughed again. He was pretty funny, but something still felt a little off to me.

"Well, I really appreciate the mirror," I said as we continued walking around the village. The villagers seemed a lot kinder to me today. Or maybe it was because Luke was standing protectively behind me like a menacing bulldog.

Throughout the day, we ate croissants and walked some more. Voss asked me several questions about myself and what life was like at the palace. He seemed genuinely curious, and I was more than happy to talk about home. I told him about Vanessa coming into the family and how much I despised her.

We began walking along the shoreline, and the villagers were following us for some reason. Every time I looked back, I saw more and more people gathering.

"Why do you hate Vanessa so much?" asked Voss out of the blue.

"How would you like it if someone broke apart your family?" I said.

A dark look came over his face, but he shook his head and covered it with a big smile.

"I understand one hundred percent."

"Come on. You can tell me," I said, chewing on the remaining piece of my croissant. "You looked like you remembered something."

"My entire family was killed," said Voss. "I would be grateful even to have one family member remaining."

"What happened?" I asked, shocked. I wasn't prepared for this type of revelation from this jolly alpha.

"Your family, the Royal Pack, killed my family," he said.

"That's impossible. Why would they do that?" I wasn't sure whether he was kidding, but his face had all kinds of seriousness written all over it. He wasn't joking in the slightest, but I didn't understand.

"It was during the Great Moon Revolt. When these villagers went under attack for supporting a sigma, they were badly attacked by the government," said Voss. "My family was part of it. Even my little brother was killed."

His voice choked up on the last sentence as he looked away from me.

"I just don't believe my family would do that stuff on purpose," I said. "It's just...unbelievable."

"So you're telling me you didn't know," said Voss, turning to me.

"I didn't know," I said in a low voice.

"Well, it's too late now," he whispered, stopping suddenly. I looked around to see why he had stopped. We were standing in front of the narrow stone path that led directly to the Shadow Wolf's cave.

"What do you mean? Why did you bring me here?"

Even as I asked the question, a sinking dread dropped like a boulder in my stomach. His resentful attitude toward my family and the full moon above us all came together. He was going to put me up for the omega sacrifice.

Ducking under the umbrella, I turned to run, but the villagers surrounded me in a small circle, pushing me toward the cave. I screamed for Luke, but I did not see him anywhere.

"Luke isn't here, my dear," said Voss evilly. And he was smiling as he gazed upon the cave.

"What did you do to him?!"

"Oh, Princess Lyra," said Voss, sticking his hand out for me to take, which I didn't. "You should be honored to be the next omega sacrifice. The Shadow Wolf is waiting eagerly for you."

"What's the point of sacrificing me?" I shouted, looking around frantically for help, holding my arms straight out and trying to block any of the Wild Wolfmen from touching me. My heart was beating wildly as I backed away slowly.

My back was to the cave, but I could see I was getting closer and closer to its entrance.

A loud howl sounded from the cave, and I froze. The howl was as chilling and paralyzing as the first day I was here.

"You will appease the Shadow Wolf," said Voss, clapping, and the people cheered. The crowd was barking and howling at my demise. "And the villagers will love me forever after this, and we will take over the kingdom."

"My family will come after you. Kodan will come after you," I threatened as they crowded me closer to the cave entrance. I turned towards the cave, horrified to see an endless dark cavern. I couldn't see anything inside it.

Where was Kodan? Did he know about this?

Voss shoved me inside when I turned my back to him. I screamed as I fell forward onto the damp cave floor, falling forward on my face. I scrambled to right myself, but my hands slipped over the slick surface.

Harsh breathing sounded to my right, and I screamed, holding onto the rock walls to stand up.

My heart pounded in my chest.

I stood still, trying not to breathe too hard or make any sudden movements, blinking several times to get used to the darkness around me. There was a rank smell in the cave, which smelled horrible, like rotten eggs.

I turned to my right and saw him.

The Shadow Wolf was in the form of a werewolf, standing tall, as high as the cave's roof. This wasn't a normal werewolf. His hairy body was enormous and towered over me. His red, piercing eyes glared at me in the dark above his large snout and dripping fanged teeth. And all around the cave were the scattered skeletons and skulls of his past victims.

Fear gripped me like nothing else.

I stood frozen against the wall, unable to move.

This was real. He was real.

Thirteen

LUKE

here was she? I had lost sight of Lyra and Voss while Voss was buying a knitted blanket.

But while looking for the princess, I was suddenly attacked by the villagers.

"Get the fuck off me!" I roared, flinging Wild Wolfmen in every direction.

One of them covered my mouth with their hairy hands, blocking me from making a noise, while three others tackled me to the ground. They had superhuman strength that I had never come across before.

While on the ground, the Wild Wolfman started grabbing me by the arms and trying to force me down.

Rain whipped in my face as I punched him, and he howled, grasping his face. Another Wolfman grabbed me from behind.

They were relentless and crawling onto me like ants.

My arms ached with fatigue as I threw him off, and then I ran out of there. I nearly slipped on the muddy banks as my legs pumped beneath me.

I needed to get to the stone tower. Kodan needed to know

what a dickwad his packmate Voss was. He would have a better understanding of what the fuck was happening.

As I sprinted to the tower, I saw Kodan fiddling with the keys to his tower, carrying a dead deer over his shoulder. Blood was splattered all over his bare chest.

The fuck. He was the definition of a sigma mountain man.

"Hello, Luke. Are you starting to trust our pack a little more with the princess?" said Kodan sarcastically, his eyes focused on the doorknob.

"No! Hell no," I shouted, out of breath, when I finally reached him. I looked behind me to see if any of the villagers followed me and saw that they didn't dare follow me to Kodan's tower.

Kodan turned to me, raising his eyebrows.

"You look shaken there. Tell me what's going on."

"Your henchman, Voss, had me attacked," I shouted, unable to calm down. Sweat beaded down my back despite the rain soaking through my black shirt. The villagers had even taken my gun. "Voss took Lyra somewhere. I have no idea where the fuck he took her."

Kodan dropped the deer with a loud squelch. His eyes widened, and his chest puffed up.

"He's taken her," he said, his mouth thinned with anger. "I told him we were done with that."

"Taken her where?"

"To the Shadow Wolf as the omega sacrifice."

"What the actual fuck?" I shouted. I began running in the direction of the ocean, with Kodan following close behind on my heels to save the princess.

Fourteen

LYRA

My heart pounded hard as my gaze locked with the beast before me. I'd never seen a werewolf that large in my life. I grew increasingly terrified, scared of what he would do.

In a split second, he lunged towards me, pinning me to the ground.

Slobber dripped from his fangs onto my chest. I quickly turned my face away, unable to look at the horror before me.

The Shadow Wolf howled, lifting his head to the roof of the cave. It sounded more like a war cry.

Something caught my eye on the wall. The word 'Cursed' was scrawled messily on the wall of the cave in red letters that looked like blood.

He didn't look like any ordinary werewolf. From my guess, he was eight feet tall, with the body of a linebacker covered in hair.

"You wrote that?" I asked frantically.

The color in his eyes shifted for a moment from angry red to brown. He looked like he was taken aback by my question.

My hand trembled as I reached out to touch his gigantic

paw lying next to my head. I swallowed, thinking about all the omegas he murdered in cold blood in this cave.

I could be next if I wasn't careful.

In a split second, his eyes shifted to red again, and he lowered his head, ripping my jacket apart with his fangs.

I screamed, and he began huffing wildly as if excited by my discomfort. His slobber spilled all over my leggings, a wide, toothy grin on his face. I screamed again when he ripped my shirt open, exposing my bra. He was growling and roaring.

Getting more and more frenzied.

I had to gain control of myself.

Taking a deep breath, I stopped screaming and touched his face instead. He stilled as I tried to project a sense of calm into him. It was no different with horses. His huffing began to cease, and his eyes began changing to a calm brown color again.

"You didn't become like this on your own," I whispered. "You were a powerful sigma."

His eyes gleamed with unshed tears. He lifted his head upward, and a long, sad howl emitted from him.

"Shh," I said, seeing his bloody ankles wrapped in chains. "Do you want me to free you of these chains?"

I sat up when he moved off of me.

I started working on the chains, unwrapping the long link around his ankles. He stood still as I untangled him. The chains were rusty and old, covered in years of blood. Or maybe it was just rust. His rank odor nearly killed me as I worked underneath him.

Maybe if I unchained him, he would leave me alone. And I could actually survive this. I didn't mind setting him on his own people. Because as soon as I unchained him, he would run.

After all, they *did* try to kill me.

Using a hairpin of mine, I was finally able to unlock his chains.

"Lyra! What the hell are you doing?"

I looked up, dropping the chains instantly upon seeing that it was Kodan. Luke was standing next to him, holding a small knife in his hand.

The Shadow Wolf crouched, dangerously free and ready to attack.

His eyes took on the fire-red color again, and he roared, charging toward Kodan and Luke. Everything happened in a split second as he knocked them both down on his way to freedom.

The Shadow Wolf sprinted off and away from the cave.

"Fuck," said Luke, groaning and rubbing the back of his head. "He's a strong bastard. And fast."

"How could you release him like that, Lyra?" asked Kodan, making his way toward me. He lifted me by the arm and inspected my body. "Are you hurt anywhere?"

"No, I'm fine," I said. "Just freezing to death in here."

"Why the hell did you unchain him?"

"He was going to kill me. I'd rather he kill the villagers and Voss, who, by the way, put me in here," I said indignantly.

Kodan sighed and sat on top of a boulder.

"The entire island of Howl's Edge is in danger," he said, covering his face with his hands, furious with me. "It's not only the villagers who will be under attack. It'll be anyone who gets in his path."

"Oh crap," I said, realizing what I had just done. My entire family was in danger, as well as innocent people.

"I'm going to hunt him down before anyone else gets to him first," he said, scratching his beard. "The Royal Pack will kill him on sight."

"Why do you care so much?"

"I care because he's my brother."

~

Kodan

LATE THAT NIGHT, I scrubbed off the deer's blood from my chest in the shower.

I couldn't think straight after this hectic day. My little brother was running around rampant and out of his damn mind.

Lyra hadn't let anyone in the bedroom for several hours with the door locked. I could tell she felt bad about what she did.

But while she sulked away, I spent that time skinning the deer and hacking it to pieces.

I had to track my brother down first thing tomorrow, but I also needed to bring my wife to safety.

When I thought about Lyra, my balls tightened with arousal. I pictured her in my mind, lying in bed in her sheer pajamas.

My dick hardened in the hot shower, and I lowered my hand, squeezing it around my dick. Closing my eyes, I pictured her soft pink pussy trembling under my fingers. I stroked up and down. Faster and faster, thinking about how her lips made an '*O*' shape when she climaxed.

I roared my release, and a load spurted from my dick.

"Damn," I muttered, my knees buckling. I held onto the walls, trying to regain control. She had power over me even when she wasn't around. I was starting to get dangerously close to her. It was supposed to be a simple marriage of alliance, but it was turning into something more.

After finishing up my shower and collecting myself, I decided to check on my omega wife. Standing outside her door, I only wore a towel around my waist. I could hear her breathing hard in there. And then I heard a moan.

Was Luke fucking her again?

But at least he wasn't planning on murdering her like Voss was doing. *Ah, Voss...*

I was going to find him and kill him as soon as I got the chance. I hadn't been able to track him after the fiasco in the cave. He enlisted the help of some of his followers to go into hiding.

I turned the doorknob and walked in.

Lyra was alone on the giant bed. She was lying on top of the blankets, with her bare knees up and her hand in the middle of her clenched thighs.

"What are you doing here?" she breathed, her eyes glazed over in desire. She had clearly been touching herself.

"Continue," I said, lowering myself onto the mattress opposite her. As I peeked between her legs, I noticed she wasn't wearing any underwear, her pink glistening pussy lips puffy and aroused. "I'm sorry for disturbing you, but continue."

"Aren't you going to leave?" she asked, biting her lip.

I lay on my side, propping myself on my elbow.

"No," I said. "I want to watch your slick seep down to your bottom. I want to watch your little pussy trembling as you finger yourself."

The princess slowly spread her knees apart, and I watched her delicious pussy lips open up before me. Her sweet scent was heavy in the back of my throat.

Arousing me. Calling to me.

She slid her finger hesitantly between her pussy lips, rubbing her clitoris in circles. Oh, how I wanted to lap up every inch of her delicious cunt. Instead, I patiently watched as she rubbed herself, taking her body to new heights. I wanted to learn what she liked. Her bare, luscious breasts bounced up and down. My cock hardened as I watched her masturbate in front of me. She writhed as she pressed her clit harder, her legs jerking open wider. She kept glancing over at me and licking her lips.

"I want your knot," she gasped, sticking her middle finger deep inside her pussy.

I wanted to give it to her. To put it inside her until I was balls deep. But I stayed quiet, watching as she finished herself. Then she sucked her fingers off in ecstasy, watching me with hooded eyes.

God, she was perfect.

Her lithe body was open and vulnerable before me. Ripe for the taking.

I dove between her thighs, brushing my tongue against her sweet cunt. The taste of her sweet honey made me unbearably hard. A moan slipped past her lips as I lapped up every inch of her pussy and her swollen bud.

"You taste so good," I growled, licking and sucking like she was my last meal. She moaned, arching her back. Her hands gripped my hair wildly as her body trembled with another orgasm as I pressed against her pussy harder.

"Lick me," she begged.

I happily obliged, sucking every drop and swirling my tongue around her nub with added pressure. "Come for me again, baby."

"Please, I can't," she begged, trying to push my face away. Instead, I added more pressure with my tongue, tasting every inch.

"Just one more. Give me that sweet honey," I said.

As I swiped my tongue up and down and around in circles, I watched as her eyes rolled back in pleasure, giving in to my demands.

Her thighs tightened on either side of my head, and my tongue slipped inside her heated hole.

"Oh my god, Kodan," she screamed. Her legs spasmed,

and her pussy released an abundance of slick, which I desperately lapped up.

Lyra

I COULDN'T BELIEVE that just happened.

I lay there spent and gasping on the mattress while Kodan lay next to me, his hand roaming my breasts.

"You're quiet," I said to Kodan.

We hadn't talked much on the way home today.

After we arrived home, I beelined for the shower to wash off the drool of the Shadow Wolf. Then, I locked myself in this room to process everything. Poor Luke was in his room, probably upset with me. I wasn't in the mood to talk to anyone after the incident.

"I don't want you to feel bad about the cave incident," he said, turning on his side and not at all furious with me anymore. "You did it to save your life. And to be honest, I don't know what I would've done if I lost you."

"Oh," I said, looking at him in a new light. He was being vulnerable and nothing like the mountain brute I had met on our wedding day.

A warmth entered my heart that he cared.

No man had spoken to me like that before. And to be honest, it felt kind of good. A cheesy smile crossed my face.

"Why are you smiling?" he asked, his lips also turning up in a small smile. "Did I accidentally say something funny?"

"No, I just think it's cute," I said. "But what's *not* cute is that you stole my pills."

He sighed heavily, his hand pausing on my belly from the lazy circles he was drawing.

"I understand now that the pills are important to you," he

said after a while. "I will return them to you. But I also have something to say."

Worry leaped in my heart. His face had taken a serious expression that I couldn't read.

"Yes?"

"If you believe in your heart that you are not meant for me," he began. "Tomorrow, I'm taking you to your parents' home. I should never have brought you into all my mess, and I need to set things right. Once I settle things here, you can either choose to stay with me or leave."

"But are you going to murder everyone in Howl's Edge if I decide to leave you?"

There had to be a catch somewhere. He was offering me freedom.

"No," he said. "I vow not to touch a single soul as long as the kingdom doesn't keep massacring the Wild Wolfmen. Or come after my brother."

"So you're not trying to trick me or anything?" I said. I couldn't believe he was doing this. He was actually being nice and letting me go.

"I would never. When have I ever tricked you into anything?" he said. "I'm not looking for an answer right now. Take all the time you need."

"I don't know what to say right now," I said, confused. I was starting to feel something toward him, but at the same time, I hated living here.

"It's okay," he said, kissing me on the lips and looking at me with a sad gaze. "I will give you some space now to think of what you want. Have a good night."

Then he got up and left the room, leaving me in the dark and alone with my thoughts.

Fifteen

LYRA

It was a bumpy truck ride home.

I was sitting on Kodan's lap like before on the back of the truck while one of the Wild Wolfmen drove.

Luke was standing at the edge of the truck, the wind making his whip around his face. He looked deep in thought, and I wondered what he was thinking about.

We were almost at the palace, and my heart raced with the anticipation of seeing my mother again. I missed her a lot while living with Kodan since I was her support after Vanessa came into the picture.

"Do you think the Shadow Wolf...I mean, your brother is here?" I asked, suddenly fearing for the safety of my family.

"He wouldn't be that dumb to show up here, but I don't think he's aware of what he's doing," he said, holding me tighter against him on his lap. I leaned my head against his chest, trying to relax. "How are you feeling, little princess?"

"I feel fine, just a little warm," I said, attributing it to the heavy fancy gold dress I wore today.

I was also highly aroused for no reason.

I was sore between my legs from being knotted by Kodan.

It was a good ache, and I craved more of it. I wanted more of him, and I felt like we should have had sex last night. My pussy tingled throughout the bumpy ride, and behind me, I could feel his hard-on pressing against me.

At least I wasn't the only one suffering, which brought me some comfort. He was trying to distance himself from me, and I was not fond of that feeling. I was used to him trying to pounce on me.

"Have you come to a decision yet? About us?"

"I haven't," I said.

The truth was that I was conflicted. I loved having Kodan near me and his raw, powerful sigma energy that brought out my soft side. I loved being intimate with him in every way. There was a potential for true love to grow if I allowed it.

At the same time, I could easily go back to the life I was living. The life of lavishness and comfort. And maybe get a second chance with a proper alpha pack.

But the last thought almost made me puke. I needed more time, and I couldn't give him an answer right then.

WALKING TOWARD THE PALACE, I wasn't expecting a parade of people cheering for me. The crowd of people grew, surrounding our vehicle.

Some of them flicked off Kodan and cursed him out. I wasn't prepared for the different reactions and volatile emotions as we walked between them towards the palace.

"Princess! Can you sign this?" begged a young girl wearing a pink tiara and a pink dress who looked about eight. She held out a fluffy diary with a pen.

"Sure," I smiled, setting pen to paper.

"What is this?" said Kodan gruffly, watching me write my name out in large cursive letters.

"Apparently, I've gained the people's trust by marrying you," I said. "It's a big deal for an omega to marry a sigma. And they know I did it to save them."

"Because sigmas are outcasts..." said Kodan. It hurt me to hear him say it. But it was true of Howl's Edge. We had a long way to go before everyone was treated with the same respect as alphas.

Reporters surrounded us, even though Luke and one of Kodan's men tried to block them off. We slowly made our way to the palace. Comments and questions peppered me from all sides. I couldn't focus anymore on any single person.

"Princess Lyra, are you happy with your new sigma husband?"

"What happened to your other alpha husband? Did Voss leave you already?"

"Did Voss not satisfy you in bed like Kodan can?"

I grabbed Kodan's hand and pulled him to a stop.

"Let's keep going," said Kodan.

"No, I want to make a statement," I said, gripping his hand as a lifeline. I grabbed Luke's hand, too.

"What are you doing?" said Luke, turning to me. He was running on adrenaline, trying to protect me, but I was hindering him.

"I want to talk to them," I said loudly over the noise of the crowd.

"Are you insane?!"

"It'll be fine, Luke."

"I'll give you a few minutes then," said Luke, giving me room to talk to them and standing at my side instead of barricading the front. A small beta woman with short purple hair shoved one of the microphones to my face.

"Princess Lyra, are you happy with your new husbands?" she asked.

"Yes, I am," I answered. "I would like to say that my sigma

husband, Kodan, has been amazing and gentle with me. I don't understand any of the hate, but he is good to his people and to me. Even though I don't come from his village, he treats me with respect."

I could feel Kodan's gaze pierce through me at my words. He was probably shocked.

I was just expressing the truth of what I felt.

"Do you prefer a sigma over an alpha?"

Honestly, the questions were starting to anger me. But I had to keep my cool.

"I think they are both amazing," I said, and the reporter's eyes widened.

"Is it true that a sigma's knot is bigger?" the reporter winked.

"Okay, this is getting out of hand," said Kodan, pulling me away from the reporters.

Luke strong-armed his way in front of us, and I followed him through the path he created. My teeth were clenched, and my body was shaking. I was literally seething inside from the reporter's lack of respect.

We walked into the palace, and when I stepped in, nervousness set into my stomach.

"Daughter!" shouted Armon, who was talking to his counselor just inches from the door.

"Hi, father," I said when he pulled me in for a bear hug.

"I was wondering what the commotion was outside," said Armon, with a concerned look in his gaze. "Is everything alright, daughter? You are not divorcing already, are you?"

"No, everything is fine," I said, patting his arm. Sometimes, I forgot how old he was getting. His goatee had gotten longer, and the wrinkles on his face were deepening. After losing one father, I couldn't bear to lose another, even though they didn't treat my mother as well as they could.

"Then what's the matter?" asked Armon.

"I have a situation to talk to you about," Kodan interjected.

"Come, come," said Armon, waving us into the palace. "Let's talk with everyone regarding this matter."

We walked into the throne room, and I saw Mother yelling at the new omega, Vanessa. Vanessa was standing there with a smirk on her face, her red hair in small curls around her face.

"You have no right, absolutely no right, to take over my closet," said Mom. "How could you throw all my clothes on the ground the way you did? No respect!"

"Listen, lady," said Vanessa, stroking her pregnant belly as if gloating. She saw us enter the throne room since we were in her line of sight. So she chose her words carefully since my father was there. We agreed that you're going to a different room. Just something a bit smaller since you're not sleeping with your husbands anymore."

I stood there shocked for a minute, then I walked over to my mom and grasped her elbow in comfort.

"What?" my mom said irritably.

Then she turned around, and upon seeing me, she collapsed into me, hugging me tightly. I could feel her tears of anger drench my dress. *Was this what she had to deal with now?*

"Just ignore her, Mama," I said. Vanessa let out a light laugh, and I saw her kiss my father before sashaying out of the room.

"I'll go get Dravin and Arther," said Armon, walking away from the situation to grab my other fathers for the impromptu meeting.

Mom broke the hug and proceeded to hug Kodan and Luke.

"It's so nice to see you all again," she sniffed. "Thank you for bringing my daughter back, even if it's just for a little bit."

"It's nice to see you too," said Luke, returning her embrace.

"Have you been nice to my daughter?" she asked Kodan with a teasing smack on his arm. He let out a chuckle, his wide-set shoulders slowly relaxing around my mother's presence.

"You should be asking your daughter if she was nice to me," Kodan teased.

"At first, everything was rocky," I said. "But we're still learning about each other."

I didn't want to mention anything about Kodan's offer—that I had a way out of the entire marriage. I didn't know how I felt about not seeing Kodan again.

"That's good to hear," Mom said. Then she turned to some of the beta servants. "Please get them something to eat and drink."

We sat on the couches in the living area, and it felt so weird to sit there. It felt comfortable, like sitting on clouds after sitting on the hard floor of Kodan's living room.

I couldn't wait to go to my room after this. I wanted to show Kodan my childhood bedroom and introduce him to a comfortable bed. Maybe that would motivate him to get us a real bed.

"We are all here now," said Armon, plopping down onto the couch across from us.

Upon seeing Dravin and Arther, my heart glowed as I hugged them both. Without Vanessa in the way, it felt like the old times. Although we weren't too close, we still talked once in a while when my fathers weren't busy with Royal Pack duties.

The servants brought us chilled water and little round sugar cookies. Everything felt like a luxury to me.

"What is happening, Kodan?" asked Dravin, crumbs of

the cookies in his beard. "Armon said you had something to tell us."

Kodan began to relay what happened in Howl's Edge and about the Shadow Wolf's escape.

"I was hoping to leave the princess here for a while until I can capture him," said Kodan. "I figured it would be a lot safer here."

Armon jumped up.

"If the beast is out there, I will send reinforcements," he declared, his goatee bobbing in excitement. His eyes were wide with the thrill of the hunt.

"That's not needed," said Kodan, nearly rising from his chair. I could hear the controlled tension in his voice. He was trying to maintain the peace with my family while protecting his own.

"I'm sure Kodan can handle it. Are you excited that I'll be staying here for a while?" I said, sensing the rising tension with my fathers, who wanted a fight with the Wild Wolfmen.

"Of course," said my mom, her face glowing.

"She'll be here just until I capture him," said Kodan. While my fathers argued with Kodan about reinforcements, I yawned tiredly. I needed to get away for a moment.

I picked up a few plates to bring them back into the kitchen.

"What are you doing, Lyra? The servants can get that," my mom said.

"It's okay. I can help out a little," I said, and my mom raised her eyebrows.

"I think living out in the village was what you needed," she said. "You've grown in just a few days."

"I guess," I laughed as I walked away to the kitchens.

Sixteen

LYRA

After dropping off the dishes, to the servants' shock, I started to make my way back to the living area. I hoped everyone was calm by then because I couldn't take the fighting much longer. I just wanted Kodan to get along with my fathers.

Walking down the long hallway covered in red carpet, I stopped and looked into the ornate mirror. My hair was a mess after traveling for hours. I quickly tried to pat down my hair as I tied it into a ponytail.

My hair still looked messy, but it would have to do.

I turned and saw Kodan down the hallway, making his way toward me. I gave him a small smile as he pulled me in for a silent hug. We didn't even have to communicate as we hugged each other for comfort.

I gasped when I felt his raging erection press against my stomach.

"What naughty thoughts were you thinking about?" I laughingly accused him.

"Just thinking about knotting you again, little princess," he said in a low voice in my ear.

Shivers swept down my spine, and I felt my panties start to get drenched with arousal. He grasped my hand in his large one, leading me away from the throne room and up the staircase.

"What are you doing?" I asked, trying to pull my hand away.

"To your room," he said. "I'm sorry, princess, but it's been hours. I need to rut you at this moment."

My pussy clenched with need. I needed him, too, but it was so inappropriate. *What if someone heard us?*

"It's not a good idea, Kodan," I said, protesting as we walked up the steps. "My parents will know."

"There's no negotiating this one," he said gruffly. "I need you open and ready for me. My cock is going to fucking explode."

"Let's go to my room," I said quickly, leading him by the hand to my room. I was horny as hell too, and maybe a quickie wouldn't hurt.

Once we were inside, I hastily locked the door with shaking fingers. This sigma wasn't waiting for anything.

Kodan pressed me up against the wall and smashed his mouth over mine. He kissed me roughly like it was going to be the last time we'd ever kiss.

Closing my eyes, I took him in.

His scent and the cologne he used this morning were intoxicating to me. His lips searched mine, kissing me with force behind it like he had been craving me.

"*Fuck*," he said against my lips. "You taste so good. I missed kissing you."

"You shouldn't have been so distant this morning," I said.

"I didn't want to manipulate your decision," he said. "Enough talking. Lift your dress. Now."

～

Kodan

I DON'T KNOW what took over me.

All I knew at this moment was to fuck my omega wife. I needed her—more than air itself.

My cock was fucking ready to erupt, and my balls were tight. I let my jeans fall to the floor as I kissed her again. Her hands surrounded me for support when I lifted her right thigh up. I pressed my other hand to the wall to steady myself as I caved her in.

I needed her tight, delicious cunt. I pressed a finger into her warm opening and found her ready for me.

"Good girl," I said out loud.

"What?" she asked innocently.

Her eyes were wide and glazed over with desire. Even though she said this wasn't right, her body said otherwise. Her breasts rose and fell with her rapid breathing as I swirled my finger around her pussy, feeling her readiness.

"My finger is sticky with your slick," I said. "Are you ready for me to go deep inside you?"

"Yes," she breathed.

"Yes, what?"

"I want you deep inside me," she breathed. She looked at the door as if worried that we were taking too long. I didn't give a fuck about the others.

I was going to take my wife when I pleased.

Removing my finger from her pussy, I pressed my slick-covered finger against her mouth as she opened her lips. She looked surprised and confused as she sucked my finger with her full pink lips.

"Do you like tasting yourself, little princess?" Her cheeks reddened with shame, but she nodded quietly. "Good girl. I like tasting you, too."

Her thigh was soft to the touch as I held her wide open for

me. She grasped my waist for balance as I inserted myself inside her. Inch by inch, her stomach flexed with her fast breaths as I pushed all the way inside of her.

Fuck.

Her pussy surrounded my stone-hard cock, enveloping it in her warmth. I slammed into her, covering her mouth as she gasped loudly. Keeping my hand over her mouth, I pulled back and then pounded into her hot, throbbing pussy.

I couldn't think straight.

I felt like I was in my rutting phase, but that was only triggered by an omega's heat—and she wasn't in heat.

At this moment, my vision was clouded, and I could only see her. My innocent omega in front of me, open and needy for me.

My cock slammed into her tight cunt repeatedly until she gasped with her own climax. Her pussy clenched tight around my shaft, sucking it deeper inside her, and I removed my hand from her lips. Instead, I covered her mouth with mine, sucking in her light gasps and breathy moans.

I bucked my hips against her once more. My cock hardened even more from the warmth of her pussy.

My cock began to tighten, getting hotter with each thrust. The heat of my semen erupted from the end of my shaft, filling her.

Every drop of my seed stuck tightly inside her. I groaned in relief as my cock swelled at the base, locking her in.

Her eyes widened in shock.

"I forgot to take my pill this morning," she said as my knot grew bigger. She tried to pull away, but she winced in pain. "I thought I was staying with my parents."

"Don't hurt yourself," I growled. "It's too late now."

I held her hips in place and carried her to the bed. It was a canopy bed with a sheer white cloth hanging down the side.

While I was still locked inside her warm opening, I gently laid her down in front of me.

"Now I won't have a real choice to leave you or not," she said, not meeting my eyes. "What if I get pregnant?"

"You can't blame me," I said. "I gave you the pills last night."

She shook her head, not wanting to see reason. Damn, she was stubborn.

"If you hadn't stolen my pills in the first place, this wouldn't have happened," she said, trying once again to pull away from my swollen cock and wincing again from the resistance.

"Breathe, just relax," I said. And apparently, that was the wrong thing to say when her eyes widened.

"How could you tell me to relax?" she said. "Okay, I know I fucked up not taking the pill, but now I could get pregnant. And your brother is running around Howl's Edge, terrorizing everyone. It's not safe to have a baby."

"You're not in heat," I said, kissing her neck and rubbing her back. I had to get her to calm down. I didn't want our relationship to end in a fight before I had to hunt for my brother and leave her here with Luke. Jealousy stabbed at my heart at having to leave her alone to bond with another mate. I knew it was the norm to share an omega, but I had never done it before. "You have nothing to worry about, little princess. Why are you crying? Tell me."

She huffed and tried to turn her face away from me. But I wouldn't let her. I grasped her chin and kissed her on the lips.

I kissed away her tears. Her pain was my pain, and I was surprised to learn that then. My heart ached when I saw her like this. I wanted to fix her pain.

"I don't want you to leave," she finally sighed against my lips once I had calmed her down with my petting and purring.

"Are you saying you want to stay with me?" I asked.

"Yes."

I stopped breathing, and I paused while rubbing her back. She actually wanted to be with me. She wanted me. Me, an outcast sigma hated by her people.

"Is that your final decision? Are you very sure?" I asked unbelievingly, gazing into the depths of her sky-blue eyes.

"I'm very sure," she said, laughing and crying. I hugged her tight, and she wrapped her shaking arms around me as my knot held her tight to me. My heart filled with warmth and pride that my omega wife wanted me.

"I love you," I said gruffly, not caring one bit if it was too early and that there was the fact that it was only days since we were married.

"Already?" she smiled, kissing me on the lips.

She didn't say it back, but I felt it in her kiss. One day, she would say it. I knew it from the deep feeling I had in my soul about her. She was the one I needed, the one I wanted, and the one I never would let go of. If she couldn't recognize it fully, that was okay.

"I'll come back for you as soon as I have the problem at home sorted," I said. "Are you willing to give up this beautiful bed and all your luxuries for a rough old sigma?"

She giggled again, pulling on the black bow tie she forced me to wear this morning alone with a dress shirt. She relented on letting me wear the black jeans with it. This morning didn't start out well for us, but then I saw hope for our future.

"Yes," she said. "Believe it or not, I don't care about this stuff anymore."

I didn't believe it, but I vowed to myself to make her as comfortable as possible living with me.

"Your room is cute," I said, looking around at the bright curtains and her books scattered on her desk. There was a large armchair with makeup supplies strewn all over it. "I take it you like to do makeup?"

"Yes," she said, her eyes lighting up. I want to open my own salon one day to help omegas on their wedding day."

She had ambitions and goals that I didn't know about. We had been too busy screwing around and not talking enough.

"Wow, I'm sure you're amazing at it," I said.

"Yeah, like when I was doing my cousin's makeup at the cafe before you barged in to destroy everyone," she said with a cheeky smile.

I groaned at the thought of ever hurting her.

"There's no need to keep remembering that," I said, kissing her on the lips to quiet her.

The knock on the door made us both jerk up, and I looked down to see us still knotted together. Her pussy was still expanded to handle my knot, pulsing around my cock.

"Who is it?" she called from the bed, pulling a blanket over us.

"Just wondering where you went," said Luke from outside the door.

"I'll be down in a minute," she said.

"Is Kodan in there with you? I can smell his scent," said Luke.

I rubbed my forehead in annoyance.

"Yes, Luke. You'll have all the days with her while I'm gone," I said.

"Sheesh, I get it," said Luke. "Calm the fuck down, sigma. Don't enjoy yourself too much, Lyra."

I rolled my eyes and turned to find Lyra smiling as we listened to his footsteps disappear down the stairs.

Seventeen

LYRA

Over the next few days, I missed Kodan. During the week, I caught up with my family and friends to keep myself busy. It was early, as I laid in bed lazily with Luke by my side while he snored soundly, his hand sprawled over my bare breast.

I had a fun time distracting myself and having mini-parties with my cousin and my friend. There were so many questions about my love life and how a sigma's knot compared to an alpha's. The answers made Beth blush, and we had an amazing time dying over her reactions.

My fathers even ignored Vanessa for a day as we watched a movie together with Mom. I knew Vanessa was seething inside the whole time, and I felt happy that Mom was happy, even if it was just for a little while.

I hadn't heard anything yet in regards to Kodan, but I hoped we'd have some news soon.

I looked over at Luke and I kissed him lightly on the cheek as I got up to take a shower. Last night, Luke had me to the point of screaming during my orgasms. It was intense and wild.

We had sex several times last night with my unquenchable omega appetite.

I lifted my feet over the bed and smiled as I looked back at his muscular naked body on the bed.

He looked like a Greek painting, sleeping peacefully. Looking at the clock, I saw that it was around nine a.m. My thighs rubbed against my sore pussy as I tiptoed to the bathroom.

The shower felt good on my heated body. For some reason, I was feeling a little bit feverish. After the shower, I had to remember to take the heat suppressant pill. I had taken it over the past couple of days, but I was starting to get worried.

I heard the creak of the bathroom door opening.

"May I join you, my princess?" asked Luke.

My heart fluttered with excitement. I couldn't get enough of him, especially after cuddling all night.

"Yes," I said while he was already parting the shower curtains. Luke was big, nearly taking up all the space in the little shower as he enveloped me in a hug under the stream of warm water. His brown hair was quickly drenched, plastered across his face as I pushed the strands away from his eyes. He stared at me, his gaze roaming across my body, staring at my navel.

I shyly covered my pussy with my hand, but his hand covered mine, pulling it away.

"Don't cover in front of me," he said, his gaze not leaving me. "Let me wash you, honey."

"I've never had someone else wash me before," I said, my hand trembling as I handed him the loofah.

"Well, I'm going to be your first," said Luke gruffly, scrubbing the loofah gently around my neck and then in circles around my breasts. "And I'm going to make sure you love it. You're going to want me washing you *every* single time."

I allowed myself to relax as he rubbed the loofah over my

belly next. My hormones were all over the place. My scent was thick, and I could see the effect it was having on him. He was concentrating on washing me, but the appendage between his legs was thick and hard, ready to plunge inside me.

Thinking about it made my pussy clench with excitement.

"You're hard," I said.

"Washing you is making me horny for you," he said, moving down to the tops of my thighs. He knelt, his giant knees on the floor of the tub as he gazed at my pubic hair. "Let me shave that for you."

He ran his fingers through the hair as I grasped the top of his head for balance.

"I can shave it myself," I protested. But he was already grabbing my shaver from the side of the tub.

"Spread your legs," he commanded. He had taken control, and I weakly spread my legs apart.

~

Luke

RUNNING my fingers through her pubic hair, I grew excited at the thought of shaving her.

But I wanted to play with her first.

I swirled soap over her pussy, using my bare fingers to massage it into her pubic hair. I could tell she was horny by how she smelled. Her scent overwhelmed the shower, causing me to want to rut her right then.

As I twisted her short blond hair, she cried out and clutched my shoulders. I loved it when she made her little noises. She was so adorable, and all I wanted to do was fuck her tight little pussy.

"I can shave myself," she said again, her breath coming out in gasps as I slid the shaver over her pussy. Back and forth, I shaved her pussy until all the hair washed off. Her bald pussy glowed in the shower, and I brought my lips to it but didn't touch it.

"Can I kiss it?" I asked, my naked body soaked with water. Water dripped over my head, but I wanted it to be covered in her slick.

"Yes."

She eagerly spread her legs wider as I lowered my mouth between her legs and gave her a big smooch right over her clit. She shuddered with arousal.

"Do you like that? Should I kiss you again?"

"Yes, it needs some love," she begged, bending her knees slightly to give me better access.

"I'll give it some love," I promised as I kissed all around her pussy, pressing my lips deep inside her center. I licked her clit, tasting her musky, sweet scent.

"God, it feels *so* good," she moaned, leaning further into me and allowing me to love her fully. I licked her folds and sucked her clit as much as possible until her legs began to shake. "I'm coming."

"Yes," I breathed against her pussy and licked her clit without abandon, pressing my tongue against her heated core. She gripped my shoulders tighter. And then she came with a loud moan, trying to close her legs.

"Turn around," I said. "I have to wash your ass."

On shaking legs, she obeyed me and turned around. I was enjoying every minute of this. It was my mission to please my omega in every way.

After applying more soap to the loofah, I stood up and washed her shoulders and back, covering her in large soapy bubbles.

"It feels so good to have someone else wash my back," she said. I applied more pressure as she arched her back. "I need a nice massage later."

"I'll massage you later," I said. "With a happy ending."

She giggled, and then I went down to her ass. Her butt was round and luscious as I dropped the loofah and grasped both her cheeks with my hands.

"Oh, you were supposed to be washing me, not playing," she teased.

"It's part of the process," I said.

I couldn't breathe as I squeezed her bottom, her skin turning pink under my fingertips. My cock hardened as I felt her delicate skin. I squeezed soap onto my hands and kneaded her with it, strawberry-scented bubbles covering her. I rinsed off her bottom and squeezed my finger between her cheeks to wash the middle.

"What are you doing?" Lyra gasped, holding onto the shower wall in front of her.

"Bend over."

"I can wash my own butt," she said, wiggling her ass in my hands.

"I'll do it thoroughly for you," I said. "I'll even shave your asshole if you want."

"Oh," she said, hesitating.

She bent down, and her smell of slick wafted to me as her pussy lips opened up again.

Kneading her ass, I slowly spread her cheeks apart and took in the beautiful sight of both her holes on display. Her virgin little asshole clenched tight as I spread her open wider with one hand.

"Your dark hole is so cute," I said, pressing my finger around her sphincter. Water dripped off the ridges as I felt her tight hole. Her hole loosened a bit for a moment, opening for me at my touch. But she quickly clenched it tight again. "Trust me. Relax for me, honey."

I continued to rub around the hole, loving the way it blinked at me. It opened and closed rapidly. When it opened again, I quickly pressed my finger an inch inside, and Lyra gasped audibly.

"It hurts a little," she said. "It stings."

She was very sensitive in her bottom. So, I slowly removed my finger.

"We'll try it again another time," I said, gently releasing her bottom. "My cock needs some attention."

She turned and smiled wickedly, going down on her knees as I stood back up. I groaned when she took the shaft of my tense dick into her mouth. She massaged my balls underneath as she swirled her tongue on the tip of my cock, licking off the pre-cum.

It felt so fucking good. My knees buckled.

"Like this?" she asked, her voice muffled against my dick in her mouth.

"Suck the tip," I commanded. When she pulled down and focused on sucking the tip of my cock, my eyes rolled back. This was the ultimate ecstasy. My balls tightened, and I couldn't hold back anymore as her tongue swirled around and around. I exploded in her mouth. She took it like a champ, sucking every drop of liquid spurting from me. "You did so good, baby."

"Why, thank you," she answered with a flick of her hair. "Are you calm now?"

"I was pretty horny when I woke up," I said, admiring the curve of her pale breasts under the water as she washed her hair. "Are you missing Kodan?"

"Just a little," she said. "If you weren't here, I wouldn't know what to do."

"Why do you miss him? You were married by force."

"He gave me a choice now, actually," she said.

I was confused. "What do you mean?"

"He said he wouldn't attack our people if I wanted to leave

him," she explained. "He offered me the choice before he left to find his brother."

"So this is your chance then," I said. "You get to have your old life back, plus me, of course."

"I don't want my old life back," she said.

What the hell?

"What do you see in him?" I asked. "I'm genuinely confused."

"Are you jealous?"

A spurt of annoyance shot through me. "No."

"I want to be with him, too," she said simply. She huffed and turned away from me. "I want to be left alone right now."

"That's fine," I said, getting out of the shower and grabbing my towel.

Every time I felt close to her, I always seemed to say the wrong stuff.

And each time, she got irritated faster. This was the time when it was good to have another mate around to appease her. Even before this marriage, we always got into small, petty arguments, but I usually ignored her until one of us wanted to talk.

Maybe she *did* need Kodan after all.

She was a different person when he was around her and a much calmer version of herself.

Eighteen

LYRA

When Luke left, a sense of foreboding settled in my stomach.

He was doing all the right things, and he cared about me. I didn't know why I always snapped at him when we became close. He had set me off with his questions, even though I was sure I wanted Kodan. I was very defensive about my relationship with Kodan when my family or friends asked me questions about him.

Later that morning, I sat with my mom and Yasmeen, eating breakfast out on the terrace. Yasmeen came over often while I was here to hang out as much as possible before I went back with Kodan and Luke to the Wild Wolfmen clan.

The red and golden leaves littered the floor, and a light breeze cooled down my coffee. It was my favorite place in the palace, where I would sit and contemplate every morning.

But my mother had a lot to say about Vanessa.

"Vanessa had taken over everything," she complained, sipping her green tea. Her gray hair was tied into a bun, her wrists flashing with dainty diamond bracelets. My mother didn't usually dress up much, but today, she wore a tighter-than-usual emerald dress that showed off her cleavage. She looked like she had gained a bit of weight ever since Vanessa showed up. I felt bad for her since she had lost the interest of my fathers after all their years of marriage. Anything could change in a split second. "Soon, your fathers will just kick me out entirely."

"They wouldn't," I comforted her. "Just talk with Vanessa instead of arguing. You have no choice now."

"She's taken my room without telling me," said Mom. "She threw out all my clothes, and now I have to stay in the smallest room in the palace. I feel entirely ashamed and embarrassed. Your fathers take her side because she's pregnant."

"Stab her in her sleep," said Yasmeen snidely while flipping back her glitter-covered hair.

"Yazzy!" I exclaimed, laughing. I looked back at Mom and saw tears welling in her eyes. Sobering up, I knew deep down this was no laughing matter.

"Sorry," said Yasmeen, also noticing the change in my mom's mood.

"If I was more careful, I wouldn't have had a stillborn," said Mom, biting her lip and staring out toward the sky. My heart ached, remembering the day I was told I was going to have a younger sibling.

"There was nothing you could have done," I said. "Don't beat yourself up over it, Mama."

"If I knew that your fathers cared so much about having another baby, I would never have involved myself with them," she said quietly. It was the first time I heard her say anything remotely close to leaving them. Even though I loved my fathers, I wanted to see my mother happy. "You girls should talk about everything with your packs. Talk about babies and all the serious stuff before things get official with a marking."

"I will," I promised, setting my coffee down on the table. I stood up and picked out a rose from the rosebush next to me.

"Where are you going?" asked Yasmeen.

"I just want to visit my little brother," I said, clutching the rose tightly in my hand. "Just need to be alone for a while, but I'll be back."

They both nodded, and I walked towards the family graveyard plot, which was quite a walk away from the main quarters. The trees were close together, forming a wall between the palace and the graveyard. The sleeve of my purple dress got caught between the trees, since I didn't want to walk around to the official pathway. I pulled my arm away, causing the sleeve to rip.

"Damn it," I said, touching the light fabric. I needed to be more careful.

I finally reached the small graveyard plot and walked to my little brother's grave with a headstone with his name, Thomas, engraved into it. Kneeling, I carefully set the rose in front of the headstone.

"I'm sorry, baby brother. I meant to visit you earlier," I whispered.

I remembered the dreadful night as if it was yesterday. It was seared into my memory forever.

The palace doctors rushed about in a panic, and I quickly threw down the eyeshadow palette that I was playing with. It was to distract myself from listening to my mother's screams of labor. I was only ten, so I wasn't allowed in the room. The makeup shattered into pieces on the floor. There was a problem with the birth. I ran down the hallway from my room to hers, watching from the open doorway.

My mother wasn't screaming anymore but sobbing quietly over a bundle of blankets in her arms. My fathers had devastated looks on their faces, staring blankly at my mother. Saku was kissing her hair, one hand over the blanket.

Scared, I walked over to my mother. No one stopped me.

"No, Lyra," said Mom, trying to stop me with her hand, but I had already seen what had happened. The baby was lying perfectly still, its eyes closed.

"Is it a boy or girl?" I asked, not sure what the fuss was about.

"A boy," said Saku. Then he pulled the blanket over to cover the baby's face from me. "He didn't make it."

"What do you mean?" I asked as tears streamed down my face.

We prepared for the baby for months. I was supposed to have a little sibling to play with. Then, my stomach twisted, and I felt sick.

The months that followed were the hardest for me.

I grasped the headstone, remembering the pain I felt every day. Over the years, the pain lessened, but I never forgot that night. Wiping the tears from my eyes, I kissed the headstone and rubbed off the sand from the engraving as the sound of birds screeched in the distance.

Sniffling, I stood up and turned.

Standing in front of the wall of trees was Vanessa. She had tears in her eyes. Had she been watching me this entire time? She quietly walked over to stand next to me and placed her hand on the headstone.

"I'm sorry for your loss," she said.

I was confused.

I didn't know how to feel right then about her. She was so weird.

"Thanks, it's okay. It's been years," I said, not sure how to reply to her. She stole my dads from my mom. She was standing there, pregnant, as if gloating over our loss. But I saw real sincerity in the depths of her eyes at this moment. She wore a red gown with sequins that flared from her hips. Her narrow shoulders and slim neck were a stark contrast to her swollen belly.

She faced the grave, tracing the headstone.

"But the pain sticks with you. No matter what you do," she said, her voice shaking.

Suddenly, I felt a hand clamp over my mouth.

I let out a muffled yell and tried to kick whoever was holding me from behind. The hand was like a grip of steel, holding me tight.

"Thank you, Vanessa," said a familiar voice.

It was Voss.

Terror shot through my body, and I struggled to escape his grip. He had thrown me to the Shadow Wolf for the omega sacrifice, and I was about to become werewolf chow again.

Vanessa turned, her eyes filled with tears at whatever demons she was battling inside.

"Let her go, Voss," she said quietly. "I've changed my mind."

Did she set me up?

"You can't change your mind now," growled Voss. "If I let her go, she'll go back and tell everyone. Then they'll have our heads for sure. You wanted her out of the way, and now you've got it."

Wait, were they conspiring to have me captured? This didn't make sense to me at all.

"Voss, we can be together, but just leave her alone," said Vanessa.

Voss laughed. "This brat will snitch. We'll be together soon after the Royal Pack is gone. First, the princess and then the rest of her family, one by one—just like we agreed, right?"

"I guess," said Vanessa, looking unsure.

I tried to bite Voss's hand, but it was plastered against my face.

"It'll happen soon enough," said Voss. "The fucking sigmas had turned soft on me. I'm the real leader of the Wild Wolfmen. Howl's Edge will be ours soon, baby."

Vanessa clutched at her dress, watching as Voss dragged me away from the palace grounds. I kicked, punched, and tried to scream, but none of that had an effect on him.

Nineteen

LUKE

I needed to make things right with Princess Lyra.

It was her choice if she wanted to be with Kodan or not. I was starting to realize that maybe I was a little jealous of her affection toward Kodan, and the more I accepted it, the easier and better my relationship with her would be.

I walked towards the terrace, where I knew she would be sitting with her mother. But when I made my way over there, I couldn't see her anywhere.

"Hello, my queen," I greeted her mother, who was sitting alone and deep in thought as she sipped the last drop of her tea.

"Luke, my son," she said cheerfully, setting down her cup. The somber expression on her oval face disappeared at the sight of me. "How's marriage with my daughter?"

"She's splendid," I said. "Do you know where she might be?"

She pointed north. "She's at the graveyard. Visiting."

"Thank you," I said, heading off toward the graveyard.

Lyra must have had a depressing chat with her mother,

which would explain her mom's sorrowful look in her eyes before I arrived. I wanted to help her. I wasn't around when she was ten and lost her brother, but she told me every painful detail she could remember.

I nearly crashed into Vanessa, who walked down the path toward me on her way back from the graveyard.

"Is Lyra over there?" I asked.

She shrugged her shoulders, walking past me with her nose in the air. *I never liked that lady.* I needed to see Lyra. It was a long pathway to the graveyard, and maybe I should have cut to the shortcut and walked between the trees.

But I wanted to give her the time she needed.

Upon reaching the graveyard, I sniffed the air. Something didn't smell right. Scanning the area, I couldn't see Princess Lyra.

She wasn't here.

A tinge of her peach scent lingered in the air. It was strong in some areas, which must have been her strong emotions coming here. Then I sensed another scent when I got closer to her brother's graveyard. It was familiar, and it evoked bad memories within me. Bile nearly rose in my throat.

It was an alpha's scent.

Another alpha had been in the area.

Vanessa was lying about not knowing anything. Vanessa's scent was all over the headstone as I sniffed everywhere. My heart pumping with adrenaline, I knew instinctively some-thing bad had happened to my innocent omega.

She was probably taken by surprise.

Running toward the palace, I went to confront Vanessa. She knew something, and she was hiding it from me. When I reached the throne room, I saw her conversing with Armon while twiddling her thumbs.

"Vanessa!" I roared, making my way over to her and wrapping my fingers around her neck. She gasped and then smirked, confirming my suspicions.

"What's the meaning of this?" asked Armon, looking back and forth between us, his hand grabbing my arm, trying to pull me away from her.

"Where's Lyra?" I demanded. I tightened my hold around her neck, and her eyes began to bulge with fear at seeing how serious I was.

"Stop...the baby," she pleaded, rubbing her stomach. I relented, loosening my hold just a little. "Let go, you fucking moron."

"Where's my daughter?" asked Armon, his eyes narrowing and his face turning red.

"She's with Voss," said Vanessa.

At the mention of his name, all I saw was red.

He had taken her again.

My hand shot out, about to strangle her, but I felt several hands pulling me back away from her. The other guards held me back as I shouted obscenities at her.

"Why is my daughter with him?" Armon asked her calmly. A coldness had set in his voice, his blue eyes ice. "He put her in danger once."

"He came and kidnapped her. I couldn't do anything about it," Vanessa replied.

She was clearly lying. I could feel it in every word. The way she shrugged nonchalantly earlier while I walked to the grave-yard was a telltale sign.

"She's lying," I snapped. Several Royal guards were holding me back from strangling that bitch. "She was quiet when I asked where Lyra was. She's hiding something, my king."

"The full truth, Vanessa," ordered Armon. "Or you will be sleeping in the servant's quarters tonight."

"Fine," she let out a long breath. "Voss and I formed a relationship. His dream was to take down the Royal Pack, and Lyra was really getting in my way when I tried to get close to you. But I never knew Voss was actually serious. I thought it was just a joke."

"Treason," said Dravin sharply. I could smell the fear emanating from Vanessa rising in the room.

"You'll be sent to the auctions after you give birth," said Armon after a long pause.

"No! How about my baby? Will my baby be with me?"

"We're keeping the baby," said Armon. "It's the final decision. You've committed a grave crime against the Royal Pack, conspiring with the enemy."

"It was a mistake," she pleaded, tears marking her face.

Then Armon turned to the guards that held me back.

"Lock her up in her room," he ordered them. They finally released me, and I flexed my arms in anger.

"Where did Voss take Lyra?" I demanded, trying to get Vanessa to focus. She had a lost look in her eyes, confused and dazed at what was happening.

I didn't give a fuck since she deserved it.

"I don't know," she said in a low voice as they pulled her away. "It's too late now."

Twenty

LYRA

"You're not getting away this time, little omega," sneered Voss as he tied my ankles with the chains used for the Shadow Wolf.

I was back in the cave.

Voss seemed determined to make sure I was sacrificed correctly this time. The macabre bones surrounding us were the stuff of nightmares, and I wondered if I was stuck in a nightmare. But the pinch on my ankles from the tight chains as Voss wound them around me several times felt very real.

"Why are you doing this, Voss?" I demanded, holding my stomach as a string of pain went through my middle. I had no idea what was happening to me, but my skin felt hot and feverish. My dress was heavy against my skin.

"The Royal Pack really thinks they're innocent," said Voss. "They need to know what the pain of losing family feels like. The Shadow Wolf will return to his lair at nightfall and find you."

I could hear cheering outside from the villagers as they eagerly awaited the beast's return. In their minds, my sacrifice would appease the Shadow Wolf for a year so he wouldn't hurt them.

"Why don't you just kill me yourself? Why go through all this?"

"The Shadow Wolf will do as I command when he realizes how loyal I am," said Voss. "You are the bait to draw him back in."

"I'm sure your little brother wouldn't be happy with this," I said.

Voss paused and touched my knee.

"He would be more than happy," he replied. "We didn't like the system and how everything was running with the Royal Pack running the island for years, especially when our best friends were sigma brothers who felt the same. The Great Moon Revolt was the greatest thing to happen on Howl's Edge. We will continue the revolt and win with the strength of the Shadow Wolf."

I had to keep him talking and maybe convince him to let me go. I couldn't sit here as bait and wait for my death.

"Why not get someone else?"

"I have to attack the Royal Pack where it hurts the most."

"It's not going to change anything," I said.

"That's it," he said, rubbing the dust from his hands and looking at the handiwork of chains tying my legs together. Then he looked at me with a devious glint in his eyes. "I think I should enjoy you a little before I go."

"What are you doing?" I asked, panicking as he knelt closer to me, bringing his mouth to my neck. He started kissing me on my neck and cupping my breasts in his hands. The smell of his cologne made me want to throw up. But the alpha energy that radiated from him pulled to the omega inside me.

I shut my eyes, resisting his pull. The invisible alpha pull was willing me to obey and relax.

"Mhm, you taste so good," he whispered, his mouth still on my neck. Then his teeth pierced my skin, and I screamed.

"No," I whimpered. "Why did you mark me?"

I felt my body stirring, awakening.

This alpha wanted me for his carnal pleasure. I felt blood trickle down my neck as he sucked. My skin was on fire, and my stomach clenched over and over in pain. My privates were throbbing with a need for relief that only an alpha could relieve.

I was going into heat, and he was triggering it.

"It's okay. You're going to die anyway," he said. "We wouldn't be mated for too long."

He smelled the air as if he enjoyed my omega scent, thickening all around us. He continued licking my neck and bit me again on my collarbone.

I screamed again, tears running down my face.

"Stop, please," I begged. "Just let the Shadow Wolf take me."

"But you taste so delicious," he said. I tried to headbutt him, but that made him angrier when he nicked me on the neck again on the same spot, deepening my wound. If he knotted me, it would seal our mating bond. I would be tied to him forever until one of us died.

A roar sounded at the entrance of the cave.

Voss removed his hold on me, and I looked up as tears blurred my vision.

My stomach dropped with dread when I saw the Shadow Wolf blocking the entrance. His hairy body filled the cave's space, water dripping from his brown fur coat. He charged toward us, and Voss jumped out of the way.

I was lying on my back on the wet cave floor, my legs tightly bound. My hands were free as I tried to crawl on my hands away from the werewolf, heart pounding wildly.

The pulse in my ears roared with my need to escape.

"There she is," said Voss, waving in my direction. "I've brought you another omega, Shadow, as I do every year. I made sure this one didn't get away."

The werewolf stopped in front of me, sniffing my legs. Then he turned towards Voss and growled, stalking him instead. My mouth dropped open in shock.

"Thank god," I breathed, watching as the werewolf charged after Voss and pinned him to the floor. It all happened in a split second when I saw the glint of a silver knife as Voss stabbed the werewolf in the chest. The Shadow Wolf howled, throwing his head back in pain.

He opened his mouth to chomp off Voss's head.

I turned my head as I heard Voss's last screams ringing in the air.

The sounds of crunching bones finally stopped, and I turned my head back to see what was happening. I was alarmed to see the werewolf lying on his back next to Voss's headless body. I averted my gaze from Voss, focusing on the werewolf.

The Shadow Wolf didn't attack me but instead saved me from my deranged husband.

Crawling on my hands, I dragged myself over to the werewolf and gripped the dagger's handle, pulling it out.

"You saved me," I whispered.

Blood dripped down from my neck onto the werewolf's fur as I pressed my hand firmly over his wound.

Something in me didn't want to let this werewolf die. I wanted him to live, regardless of his deadly past.

"Please wake up," I said, tapping his fur-covered face. My skin heated even more as I pressed tightly against his wound, and my scent covered the entire cave in my desperation.

"He's dead," said a voice behind me. It was Kodan, and he sounded resigned. Luke barged in as well in his werewolf form.

"No, he can't be dead," I said stubbornly, trying to stop the blood as I held on.

My heart ached as I looked at his face.

He was doomed to be stuck in this werewolf form forever. Then something took over me, and I kissed his cheek, trying to ignore the stench of blood and death. I closed my eyes, pressing my mouth against his cheek, focusing on projecting life and love into him. I imagined the sandy beach of Howl's Edge and the twinkle of stars at night. My calming omega energy flowed through every inch of my body.

Suddenly, a glow emanated from his fur. The cave lit up in an orange light.

I stared, astonished, as the fur started to retract from his body and his bare skin began to show. His body began to shrink into a normal-size sigma body. Long, curly black hair flopped over his face, and his fangs retracted, revealing a nicely sculpted jawline and mouth.

He looked similar to Kodan, but a younger version.

"Impossible," said Kodan as Luke was busy untying the chains around my ankles, but he also stopped to look.

The Shadow Wolf opened his eyes and sat up in his naked form. His gaze immediately turned to me, looking at me with shock and wonder. His wound began to heal in front of me as he finished shifting.

"I am forever indebted to you," he said, his voice hoarse. He put a hand to his throat. "It hurts to talk. It's been years. What is your name?"

"My name is Lyra," I answered, glad that he survived. I couldn't believe such a werewolf could turn into a hunky–but hot–sigma. My heart pounded hard as I also locked eyes with him. "And you're welcome. You saved my life first."

"I'm Seth," he said quietly.

We looked at each other for a couple of minutes, and he leaned in.

"Seth," interrupted Kodan, stretching out his hand and pulling his brother up to his feet. Without words, they hugged each other, and tears sprung to my eyes. Luke shifted back into alpha form and helped me stand up.

He hugged me while the brothers tried to catch up.

"Let's get out of this fucking cave," Luke muttered, staring at Voss's body.

When we stepped out of the cave, we stood at the entrance. The villagers were on the other side of the narrow bridge, watching us. Then, one by one, the fur disappeared from their bodies, revealing naked bodies everywhere. They looked down at their bodies in shock, and I looked toward Kodan, who was grinning.

Cheers and clapping resounded through the crowd, and Kodan kissed me on the lips.

"You saved them. You saved us all," he said, and my mind whirled. "The curse is broken, and they can live normally again."

Everything seemed to be moving in slow motion for me. Dizziness overtook me, and I collapsed against Luke.

Then everything went black.

Twenty-One

KODAN

At the hospital, my omega princess looked frail, hooked up to so many wires.

We had been here the entire night, and she finally woke up an hour ago, muttering intelligible things before falling back asleep. The doctor said she had lost a substantial amount of blood and that they needed to keep an eye on her.

Bandages surrounded her neck from where the bastard had bitten her. I wished Seth would have at least given me a chance to kill the traitor, Voss.

Luke, Seth and I somberly sat in chairs lined up on one side of her bed while her mother and King Armon sat on the other side. After Lyra fainted, we rushed to the mainland for the hospital, and thankfully, we got there in time.

The long ride was the most harrowing trip of my life as I held her in my arms. I wasn't sure if she had very long to live, and I had never been so terrified in my life.

She had grown on me.

I didn't realize how deep my affection ran for her until she collapsed in Luke's arms. At that moment, my heart stopped like I had been stabbed. And that was when I knew. She was for me, and she was my omega.

I held her hand gently, watching her breathe peacefully on the hospital bed. Wisps of her blond hair lay messily around her face, flowing down her shoulders. She wore the blue patient gown over her body, which was doing nothing to cover her from the chilly room.

"Is there a blanket somewhere?" I asked the nurse, who was busy scribbling things onto her clipboard.

"For you?"

"For her," I said, looking at the goosebumps on Lyra's legs. The nurse looked annoyed when handing me the blanket, but I didn't care. I tucked the blanket around Lyra's body, ensuring she was warm and comfortable.

"You really care about her," her mother, Queen Ophelia, observed as I tucked in my omega.

King Armon refused to talk to Seth, my younger brother, due to their bloody history. The room was filled with strained silence. Luke was chewing on crackers, the package held loosely in his hand as he gazed upon our wife's face.

"He does," said Armon. Then he looked at Seth. "But I don't know about that one."

"She saved my soul. I care about her, too," said Seth. I let out a breath, grateful he didn't take the bait since he was a hothead growing up.

"But why are you here, though? Don't you know she's the princess, part of the Royal Pack?" said Armon, not letting it go and making this an awkward moment. I saw Seth sit up straighter in the chair, his jaw tensing.

His face reddened in anger.

"Do you still think you're better than everyone else? Torturing my father until he died?" he burst out, standing up and knocking the chair back with a crash.

"Seth!" I growled, grabbing his arm.

He was a lot stronger after being trapped as wolf for many years. Muscles bulged from his arms, and I wasn't sure how long I could hold him back if he attacked. I was angry at the king as well, but I had learned to temper it.

I had nothing but contempt for her fathers and how they operated the island. For years, I had wanted to enact revenge.

"You needed to be punished," said Armon calmly, sitting in his chair nonchalantly.

"But my father didn't do anything. He was innocent!" shouted Seth.

Seth lunged over the bed, pulling out of my grasp. Before he could reach Armon, the princess stretched out a small hand and touched his arm. His demeanor suddenly changed at her touch, the fire in his eyes dissipating.

"Are you okay?" she asked in a low voice, her blue eyes wide with panic seeing his body crouched over the bed.

"I need some air," he rasped, stalking out of the room without another glance at anyone.

∼

Lyra

WHAT WAS GOING ON?

When I opened my eyes, the bright lights in the room nearly blinded me. Mother was sitting to my right, her face breaking into a wide smile upon seeing me awake.

I woke up briefly earlier, thinking that I was stuck in a nightmare. My body was covered in sweat from my heat. Shivering, I pulled the blanket off, grateful for the cool chill in the room.

"What happened?" I asked, looking around at the men surrounding me.

Luke gave me a one-armed hug.

The smell of his cologne caused a wave of desire to sweep through my entire body. Remembering I was in heat, I wanted to tell them what was happening to me, but my parents were right there.

"Nothing, daughter," said my dad, Armon. "Just the little sigma brother acting out."

"He has every right to be upset with you," Kodan interjected, balling his hands into fists.

"What are you all talking about?" I said, still feeling a bit woozy from my drugs.

"Nothing to worry your little head about," my father said in a loud voice, standing over Kodan.

Kodan equally stood up on the opposite side of the bed. They rounded my bed, and my heart rate increased from the sound of the heart monitor next to me.

"Whoa, there," said Luke, trying to get between them.

"The only reason I'm not killing you right now is because of your daughter," said Kodan.

"If my daughter had a choice, she'd leave you at this very moment," shouted Armon. "Try it. I will kill every last one of your men."

"Dad, stop, please," I tried to say loudly, but my voice came out in barely a whisper. I tried to sit up, but my mother held my shoulder down.

"They'll sort it out," my mom whispered, her eyes wide as she watched.

"Your daughter wants to be with me," said Kodan, his lips pulled back in a snarl. "She's my wife, after all."

"Do you want to be with this idiot?" my dad asked me. "If not, I'll give the orders to execute."

"Dad, stop," I pleaded. "Of course I want to be with him."

"Lyra, he's not good for you."

"He's good to me, dad. Please stop this," I said, exerting the last of my energy to calm him.

"I think it's time our visit is up," said Armon, grabbing his wife's hand. He was clearly unhappy with my answer.

"But Lyra," my mom protested, looking back at me. My dad huffed and looked like he regretted being rude to me.

He walked to my side of the bed and kissed my forehead.

"Do you feel okay, sweetheart?" he asked, looking me in the eyes with concern. I knew he cared about me, but being in the same room as Kodan was hard for him.

"It's just a scratch," I said, touching the bandages on my neck. "I feel a little tired, but I'm fine."

"You're our princess warrior. We'll be heading out for now, but we will visit you later," he promised.

"Alright, bye," I said as they hugged me. They left the hospital room, and I let out a long sigh.

I had no idea what happened between Kodan, Seth, and my dad, but I didn't want to get involved.

All I could concentrate on now- was how my body was feeling. I couldn't get cool enough as I squirmed on the bed in pain. My skin was hot and flushed. I was throbbing between my legs, like something was missing.

"What's wrong, my love?" asked Kodan, watching me as I fidgeted and squirmed on the bed.

"Pain in my belly," I gasped. "And a strange feeling of emptiness..."

"I think she's in heat," said Luke in a low voice.

"This is not supposed to be happening," I said, holding a hand between my legs to temper my aroused senses. The only people in the room were Kodan and Luke on each side of my bed. "I even took the heat suppressants."

"When did you take it?" asked Kodan.

"I don't know," I said, confused. My brain was a jumble ever since we saved his brother in the horrible cave. "Either way, I need help."

"We need to wait until you're discharged from the hospital," said Luke, rubbing my knee. I ached for that hand to move up a little higher, to finger me senseless and then fill me with his thick alpha knot.

"I can't wait that long," I begged.

Kodan leaned down and put his mouth to my ear. "Believe me; I'd rut you senseless right now if you were in full health and not in the hospital."

I clenched my thighs at his words as a drop of slick dampened my panties.

The curtain to the room slid open, and the nurse wheeled in a tray of food. My stomach growled, and Luke chuckled, hearing it. When the nurse left, Luke picked up the bowl of food and a spoon.

"You need to eat," Luke said, holding a spoonful of mashed potatoes to my face.

"I can't," I protested. "I need a knot right now."

"I will put my finger inside you while Luke feeds you," said Kodan at last. His eyes darkened with desire as he gazed at my body. "Does that work, baby?"

"Yes," I panted, spreading my legs for his thick fingers. I desperately needed some kind of relief.

His hand disappeared under the sheets. His warm hand rested on my thigh underneath the hospital gown. The heat on my skin increased, sensitive to his every touch as he rubbed me in circles.

"I will put one finger inside you if you take a bite," ordered Kodan. "Open your mouth for Luke."

"Fine," I said, opening my mouth as Luke fed me a spoonful of mashed potatoes. While the food was in my mouth, Kodan inserted his thick middle finger inside my wet channel. My pussy clamped tight around his finger as I swallowed the mashed potatoes. The soft, gooeyness of the potatoes was delicious against my tongue. "More."

As I took another spoonful, Kodan pushed in a second finger inside me, stretching me wider.

"Good girl," Kodan praised.

Seth

I WATCHED Armon and his wife from the parking lot as they drove away.

The Royal Pack didn't deserve to live after what they did to my father.

Standing by the corner of the building, I couldn't tear myself away from the omega princess inside. I couldn't explain it. Since the moment she touched my werewolf paw, there was a pull she had over me. No omega was brave enough to do that.

She was the only reason I didn't destroy her family.

The entire Royal Pack was responsible for many deaths. Sigmas were treated like outcasts, so I had peacefully protested for years until they decided to imprison my father. When my father was taken, I ramped up more support, and the protests became deadlier on both sides. We were being picked off. The day my father's death was announced was the day I lost it. I never forgot the crying mothers and the dying beggars as I commanded my men to attack Howl's Edge.

And it was the exact day I was cursed by the island witch.

"No omega will ever love you. You will be doomed to stay forever in this form until your death," said the witch.

And yet, in my heart, I felt that the omega inside the hospital was my fated mate.

Twenty-Two

LYRA

Kodan's fingers continued to pump inside me when I finished the last bite of the mashed potatoes.

"Drink," said Luke, and I sipped from the straw he offered me. The water was cold and delicious against my parched throat. Swirls of heat centered in my core as Kodan continued fingering me.

Slick was seeping down my thighs, coating his hand. The more I thought about it, the more heated I became.

Kodan's brother, Seth, entered the room. His curly black hair was cut short, and he wore a black shirt with blue jeans. His shirt clung tight to his chest, outlining his six-pack muscle tone.

His eyes roamed over my open naked legs, barely covered with the hospital gown with Kodan's three fingers deep inside of me and Luke feeding me. His eyes widened, but he simply stood on the end of the bed, watching.

When his eyes lowered to my pussy, I felt ashamed and tried to close my legs.

"Don't stop on my account," he said gruffly. His gaze was fire against my skin, lighting me up even more.

I kind of enjoyed having an audience while I was being pleasured. I looked up at Kodan, who winked at me, pumping his fingers even faster.

The heat in my core pulsed and intensified.

My stomach clenched, and I moaned loudly as my thighs shook uncontrollably. I clenched my legs tight around his hand, but his hand blocked me from shutting him out completely. I couldn't take it anymore. He kept on pumping with his three fingers, taking me to new heights. Then he lowered his head to my pussy, sucking on my clitoris with his wide tongue. Loud, wet suction noises sounded in the room, causing me to orgasm again.

I stuffed my hand in my mouth to keep from screaming and alerting all the nurses.

After a few seconds, I caught my breath as Kodan quietly slipped his fingers out, licking off my slick from his fingers.

I quickly pulled the sheets over my body to cover up in front of Kodan's brother. He shouldn't be here, and I felt guilty getting off from his blatant stare at my pussy.

I started to grow angry at Kodan for not stopping his brother from staring at his naked wife.

"Why were you watching me?" I asked Seth. I needed answers. He scratched his head, looking between Kodan, myself, and Luke.

"I'm your mate too," said Seth, his stare holding my gaze.

What?!

I tried to look away, but I couldn't. My heart was beating so fast at this moment. I couldn't handle Luke and Kodan, who barely got along.

"No, you're not," I said. "You're joking."

But even as I said it, I felt like something was wrong. Something felt empty in my heart as I tried to reject him. His dark gaze seemed to look through my soul, and I knew instantly that he was right.

Kodan squeezed my shoulder.

"Seth is my brother," said Kodan. "He will be part of my pack, which means he's your mate as well. Will you accept him as your mate?"

Biting my lip, I looked back at Seth, and he quietly grasped my hand in his. The flutter in my heart told me all that I needed to know.

"It probably sounds crazy, but do you feel the connection, too?" Seth asked.

"I do," I said. "But I need some time. I want to get to know you first."

"Take all the time you need," he assured me.

"Then I accept you as my mate," I swallowed. I wasn't sure if I was doing this correctly at all. I knew that I felt something toward him back in the cave. Even before he shifted into his normal sigma form, I felt a connection with the beast.

"May I kiss you?" he asked.

I nodded, giving him a small smile, and he lowered his face to mine. His lips pressed against mine, and flutters descended to my core. He also had a muted scent similar to Kodan's but with an undertone of earthy scents, like a fresh garden. His face was shaved, but his sideburns prickled against my skin. Closing my eyes, I took in his scent, my heat worsening.

THE NEXT DAY, I was finally cleared to go home.

There wasn't an exact reason why I fainted yesterday other than the fact that I had lost a ton of blood. The intense, stressful situation of getting kidnapped may have played a part.

After taking a shower at the hospital, I slowly pulled on a clean pair of underwear and a bra that my mom had brought for me yesterday.

I did my hair in the bathroom, enjoying my alone time away from their intense gazes. Seth and Luke waited for me in the room, and Kodan had left early to procure transportation for us. Somehow, being in the room with an alpha and two sigmas made the heat worse. My body would crave their touch and affection, with the end goal of their knots inside me.

I twisted my hair into one long French braid, careful not to touch the bandages on my neck. Voss had not only bitten me; he'd ravaged my neck. I was scared to see the damage he'd done to me. It was still painful, but the pain medicine was helping me through it.

Walking back into the room, I noticed Luke standing at the window, looking out at the street. Seth wasn't in the room. We were in a high-rise building overlooking the island's beautiful view. His gaze automatically fixated on me as I entered the room, and my face heated. I only wore my bra and underwear. I grabbed the dress that was hanging next to my hospital bed. It was a light summer blue dress that my mom also brought. As I put it on, I was grateful it was thin and not too heavy on my heated skin.

"I can help you," said Luke, zipping up my dress from the back. His warm fingers paused on my shoulders, and he kissed my cheek while he stood behind me. His nearness and scent nearly made me go crazy with lust. Instead, I took a few deep breaths and relaxed against him, reaching up to grasp his fingers in mine.

"I'm sorry about the other day," I said, talking about the morning after we took a shower together.

"Don't worry about that," said Luke. "I forgot already, and I shouldn't have pushed you like that with my questions."

"We're going to start a whole new life," I said. "With two sigmas."

"They're not all that bad," said Luke. "I was raised close-mindedly like the rest of the island, viewing sigmas as outcasts.

But Kodan is more alpha than three alphas put together, and I respect him for that. He cares deeply about you."

He was right.

Every day, I felt the connection between me and Kodan deepening.

"He said he loved me," I blurted out. I turned around and saw that those words didn't sit well with Luke. Damn it, I should have kept that to myself. Sometimes, I saw Luke as a friend and still confided in him. But I had to remember that he was my husband, too.

"That's good," he finally said. Then he met my eyes. "I've always loved you, too. You know that, right?"

I was taken by surprise. "I love you too, Luke."

The door opened, and Seth poked his head into the room. "Are you ready, Princess Lyra? Kodan is ready with the car out front."

"I am, but you can call me Lyra," I said. His face twisted into a sly smile.

"Good to know we're getting closer, then," he commented, and my face heated. "I'm not just an acquaintance anymore."

"You're getting there," I giggled.

"Wow, you actually got us a normal car," I exclaimed, sitting in the backseat of the air-conditioned car between Kodan and Seth. Luke had volunteered to drive. It felt way nicer sitting here than in the back of a truck. As we pulled out from the hospital, Kodan rested his hand on my left knee. There was a crowd of people waiting outside, cheering upon seeing us. "What are they doing?"

"They're cheering for you, baby," said Kodan. "If you

hadn't noticed, they are the Wild Wolfmen. They've been slowly moving back onto the mainland of Howl's Edge."

I saw reporters taking pictures of the car and trying to peek inside.

"Great, the reporters won't be shy about following us now," said Luke. "Seth, are you able to shift between forms? Could you quickly shift into the Shadow Wolf and give them a quick roar?"

"Unfortunately, I can't," Seth laughed. "As much as I tried, I couldn't shift back into wolf form. It was miserable anyway."

"Would be great to put it to use and scare off these people," grumbled Kodan, gripping my knee tighter. His touch sent a wave of desire ignite through me. The ache down there worsened as I sat between Kodan and his brother. I gripped both of their thighs, pulling them closer to me.

"The heat is getting worse," I said, even though I was in the direct line of the air conditioner. "I need relief."

"Just hold on for a while longer, little princess," said Kodan, trying to purr into my ear and calm me.

"If there were enough room in the car, I would have knotted you by now," said Seth matter-of-factly. Clenching my thighs together, I couldn't help but produce more slick as my mind raced with what we would do when we reached home.

Twenty-Three

LYRA

Later that night, we finally arrived at the stone tower.

The stars shone in the night sky as we walked towards the looming building. It was a quiet night, and barely any villagers were left on this side of the island. Most of them had left for better opportunities and a second chance. There were a few straggling merchants moving shop, packing everything up. Once in a while, I would get an occasional hug from one of them, thanking me for saving them. I honestly didn't feel like I saved anyone, since I mainly fought for my life in the cave of horrors.

The air smelled like rain, and thunder rumbled in the distance just as I was thinking it.

"It's about to rain," I said, looking up at the sky.

The rain started to come down on us, and I ran towards the front door.

"Shit," said Kodan, dropping the keys. My hair was starting to get drenched.

"You're so clumsy," I joked. I was in a good mood. I had just gotten out of the hospital, and I was finally going to get some relief tonight from this dreadful heat.

"There," he said, opening the door as we all piled inside the home.

Upon looking at the living room, I gasped. I saw a brand new white leather sectional and a TV in front of it.

"What happened here?" I asked, shocked.

Kodan wrapped his arm around me. "I wanted to surprise you. While looking for my brother, I had some spare time."

"No wonder you never found me," Seth mocked.

"Quit being a smart ass," retorted Kodan. "At least I wasn't murdering omegas in a cave."

"Ah, low blow there," said Seth, wincing.

"I want to get changed," I said, interrupting them before it became a blown-out fight.

When I reached the main bedroom, my eyes widened upon seeing the brand new alpha-sized bed with a wooden frame, and next to it was a circular-shaped cushion covered in pink sheets. Even though the nest looked haphazardly put together, I was still touched by the gesture. I sat in my little nest, sinking into the soft cushion.

"Do you like it?" asked Kodan, sneaking up behind me.

"That's all I ever wanted," I said, nearly in tears, hugging him around the waist. He touched my hair, his huge palm nearly covering half my head. "It'll do for now until we can move into a nicer home."

"What?" he asked, taken aback.

"I love everything," I said. "But it's too small to raise a family in. Like when we have babies."

"Did you say babies?" asked Kodan with a hitch to his breath.

"Yes," I breathed.

"I will look for a proper home immediately," he promised. "But for now, are you happy here?"

"I am," I said, standing on my tiptoes to kiss him. He pulled me in for an embrace, kissing me hard on the lips. My stomach clenched painfully, and I doubled over. The heat was progressing faster than I expected, expelling the lining of my womb. Slick covered my thighs, and I moaned in pain.

Kodan lifted me in his arms and gently settled me on the bed. Luke and Seth were already at my other side, touching my breasts, arms, and legs.

My vision was starting to get fuzzy as my womb clenched repeatedly. Only a knot could stop the painful clenching of the belly. If an omega waited too long without any medicine or help, she could die. There were even emergency centers where alphas were on-call to help an omega in heat.

"Take deep breaths," Luke instructed, cupping my right breast over my dress, his mouth on my ear. I didn't realize I was hyperventilating as I took a few deep breaths.

"It's so painful," I cried out when another spasm of pain flashed through my center.

∼

Kodan

WE HAD DELAYED KNOTTING her for too long.

I regretted risking that, but I was going to make it right. I turned her on her side and unzipped her dress.

I pulled it down over her arms and down her body. Seth grabbed the end of it, throwing it on the floor.

She needed us urgently. I could see it on her face. Her eyebrows furrowed in pain, and her breaths came as fast gasps through her clenched lips. Her white underwear had a large wet stain on the seat of it. Gently, I pulled her underwear down over the heated skin of her thighs.

Seth held her thighs open for me as I quickly got to work, removing my belt and pants.

"Everything hurts," she sighed, her face pink and flustered.

Her blond hair lay in curls around her face. "I need a knot. I need one of you right now."

"Don't worry," Seth tried to comfort her. "Kodan is going to knot you first. We will take care of you, Lyra."

I ripped my shirt off, impatient to give her some relief. It was all my fucking fault for delaying, and she was in a lot of pain. I knelt between her thick, creamy thighs, noticing she had put on a little weight while I was gone.

She looked so delicious.

It was probably the little cakes she loved to indulge in at the palace. That little fact endeared her to me even more as I gently squeezed her thighs.

Spreading her apart wider with my knees, I noticed her patch of blond hair covering her pussy. Running my fingers through it, I felt the slick that coated her little hairs.

Her pussy lips spread alluringly open for me, inviting me.

Rubbing my cock all over her entrance, I soaked it in her slick before I could plunge it inside her waiting pussy. Her chest rose and fell rapidly, awaiting my entry as I rubbed my dick around her pussy and her swollen clit.

"I'm going inside you now, princess. Are you ready for me?"

"Yes, Kodan," she breathed, widening her legs. Her pink pussy was on display for all the men to see. Without wasting another second, I plunged inside her, and her lips rounded in surprise.

Stuffing my thick rod inside her tight pussy, I began to rock my hips against her, pushing my cock all the way in. The dimly lit room didn't hide my omega's facial expressions as she looked at me longingly, needing release. Her nails dug into my back as I thrust in and out of her.

Then I began to speed up. My balls couldn't take the tension anymore.

I fucked her senseless as I thrust wildly in and out, slamming into her pussy as my cock hardened with every thrust. I could feel the pre-cum drip from the end of my cock directly into her womb.

Moons, her pussy was so sweet and tight.

I roared my release, shooting semen inside her as my balls tensed. Her shouts joined mine as she orgasmed at the same time around my cock. Her pussy throbbed and clenched around my dick, milking me dry.

Collapsing next to her, I pulled her to me, hugging her tight as my cock knotted deep inside of her, locking her.

She opened her eyes and gave me a coy smile.

"What is it?" I growled.

"I like seeing you lose control," she said, staring at me with a new light in her cornflower blue eyes.

"You make me lose control," I replied, kissing her square on the lips as she snuggled into my knot and wrapped her leg around my waist. "Do you like my knot inside of you?"

"It feels so good," she said, pushing herself tighter against me to push it in deeper.

It felt amazing to lie with my wife again after being separated for so long. I absorbed her smell and her essence as she snuggled in over my knot.

Lyra

It wasn't long before I craved the next knot in line.

After Kodan's knot released me, I took a five-minute break to use the bathroom, and by the time I got back, my heat was intensifying again. I wasn't prepared for how intense these heats could be, but I heard it was different for every omega.

"How long do you think I'll be in heat?" I asked, snuggling between Luke and Seth. Kodan hopped into the shower, especially after spending time at the hospital.

"I would say a week," said Seth, rubbing my back as he spooned me.

In front of me was Luke, lying lazily on his back, his cock erect in his briefs.

"If you all weren't here, it would be horrible," I said, feeling the deep ache in my belly again. I grasped Luke's penis from outside his boxers, and his eyes widened in surprise.

"I thought you needed a break," said Luke.

Seth's hands dipped lower, cupping my ass. "You have a beautiful body. Do you care if I play with your ass while Luke pounds into you?"

"I don't mind," I said, scared because I never had anything go inside my ass. I found the opening to Luke's boxers and slipped my hand inside, grasping his bare member.

Squeezing my fingers around it, I rubbed up and down as he groaned.

"You're going to make me cum before I even get inside you," he said, stopping my hand with his. He turned on his side and grasped my leg, lifting it over his waist. He rubbed his fingers against my pussy and lifted his drenched fingers to his nose, sniffing me. My face turned hot. "You're more than ready."

I was throbbing as he slowly pushed himself into me. Seth was squeezing and massaging my butt.

Luke's cock stretched me wide as the full length of it struggled to get inside. I was still a little sore from Kodan, but I stretched my leg higher, giving him more room. I was breathing hard by the time his entire cock was inside me.

I clenched tight around him as he began to thrust while lying next to me. Seth's hands began to spread around my butt, and I felt his face prying around down there. Then, his nose began to press against my hole.

"Seth, what are you doing?" I gasped.

"Don't worry about me," he said slowly as he explored my behind. I felt instantly self-conscious, clenching and trying to block him. But he continued to rub his nose directly between my ass cheeks.

Luke's thrusting soon overpowered what Seth was doing, grabbing my attention again. He turned my face to him, holding my gaze to him.

He wanted me to focus on him at this moment.

And I did.

I grasped onto his muscular arm from all his bodyguard training. His cock stretched every crevice of my pussy, opening me up for him. His arms flexed as he pulled in and out. His hips flexible and fluid like a panther.

"Oh, Luke," I gasped when he pistoned hard into my eager pussy. He growled as his eyes darkened with lust, and squirts of hot semen streamed inside me while his knot locked me in place. Seth released my bottom, and I was relieved he didn't do anything further to my ass.

"I love you," said Luke, kissing the bandage on my neck, and tears fell uncontrollably down my cheeks. He wrapped his arm around me, hugging me. "What's wrong, baby? Does your neck hurt?"

"I thought you felt forced...obligated to marry me," I said. He was silent for a moment.

"In the beginning, it felt a bit like that," he admitted. "But it wasn't long after that I realized I'd been denying my true feelings for you. Lyra, you are one of a kind."

He rubbed the tears from my eyes as I sniffled.

"I'll get a bath going for you," said Seth, and I nodded. While Seth went off to fill the bathtub, I cuddled with Luke until his knot would release me.

"Well, I'm glad you feel that way now," I said. "I love you too, Luke."

His eyes lit up, and we kissed. Making out on the bed after being knotted was the best feeling in the world for an omega. Or maybe it was just me. Something about it made me feel secure, loved, and protected.

153

Twenty-Four

SETH

The naked princess looked delicate and frail as she stepped into the bathroom. She looked surprised to see me still there, waiting for her. I touched the water, which filled the bathtub to the brim.

Good, it was still warm.

"You put rose petals in the water," she smiled, stopping in front of it.

"I did," I said.

"Are you going to sit there the whole time?" she asked, licking her lips and watching me with uncertainty. I cocked my head to the side as if thinking about it.

"Yes," I said. "Should I leave?"

"No, not at all," she said hastily, stepping into the bath. She closed her eyes in delight as she soaked into the warm water.

I was admiring her dainty legs and prim breasts.

I haven't been with a female since I was turned into a wolf. Being in the presence of this omega was enough to make me go crazy. My cock was hard as I gazed at her feminine curves of beauty. She was like a masterpiece. The smell of her heat was triggering my rut, and I had to quell the urge to fuck her right then while she was alone in the bathroom with me.

I got up and shut the door behind her, locking it. Making it even more intimate.

When I turned back to her, the bubbles barely covered her chest. Her breasts jutted above the water, her nipples pebbled. She reached up, touching her neck.

"I think these bandages are ready to come off," she said, catching me looking at her. She reached up to pull one off, and she winced.

"I'll help you," I said, leaning over her and soaking the bandages in water before quickly removing them. The bite marks had stopped bleeding, but there was still a long gash against the back of her neck, which was still healing. Anger bubbled in my chest at the sight of the long red streaks on her neck.

I didn't get to her in time.

"Thank you," she said. Her soft voice calmed my response to seeing the scars on her neck.

I took a deep breath as I threw the bandages away. I perched on the toilet seat, watching her as she delicately poured soap on a sponge. She began to wash her arms leisurely, leaning back into the tub.

"Why weren't you scared of me?" I asked her. "In the cave and even now. Omegas shouldn't be with sigmas."

"Because I know you were meant for me," she said slowly, her long, dark eyelashes lifting as she looked at me. Her gaze was sultry...seductive, even. And she had no idea the effect her every move had on me. "I was scared at first in the cave. But I could see you were trapped, and it was in your eyes. I can't explain it."

"I know," I said, feeling the same when I looked into her eyes in the cave. I felt a sense of safety and comfort. I reached out, holding my hand out for the sponge. "May I?"

"Yes," she said softly, handing it to me, and our fingers brushed.

The slightest touch sent my cock into fucking overdrive.

Dipping the sponge into the water, I softly scrubbed against the back of her neck and shoulders. She stretched her neck, seemingly enjoying the massage.

"I can give you a real massage after your bath," I said.

"I would love that," she replied.

The thought of her lying on her stomach, with her naked butt in the air, played havoc on my mind. I couldn't wait, and my sack below was tense and ready to impregnate this omega in heat. I wanted to knot her so hard until she was satisfied. *To be so deep inside her glorious pussy...*

Washing her breasts next, I circled the sponge around each orb, allowing the soap to run down to her pebbled nipples. She gazed up at me and touched my face, playing with my sideburn while I worked the sponge around her boobs.

"How old are you?" she asked.

"Thirty-four," I said. "Does that alarm you?"

"No. You're younger than Luke and Kodan."

"Good, because I plan on sticking around," I said, washing her stomach next. Then, I dipped the sponge lower between her legs. "Please spread your legs. I need to scrub your pussy."

Her face turned pink as I pressed the sponge between her legs, making sure to press between her pussy walls. I needed her squeaky clean for the massage later.

"You're turning me on again," she whined, trying to close her legs, but that only served to push the sponge harder against her pussy.

"I need you horny for what I have planned for you," I said.

Lyra

AFTER MY BATH, Seth walked me to the bedroom while I had a towel wrapped around my body. Seth had surprised me with his gentleness and efficacy in a new relationship. He wasn't overbearing, and he sensed whenever I felt uncomfortable. The new bed was already mussed, with the white blankets lying around everywhere.

"One sec," he said, making his way to the bed and stripping the mattress bare. I could hear Luke and Kodan conversing downstairs. Their thick voices resounded through the tower. "Lay right there. In the middle."

With the fluffy towel still wrapped securely around my breasts, I lifted myself onto the bed, and he helped lay me face down. I laid my head to the right, watching as he grabbed oil from the nightstand.

Then his large hands were on me, unwrapping the towel-exposing my entire backside. After being knocked around in the cave, I couldn't wait for the massage.

"Thank you for thinking of this," I said, wiggling into a comfier position on the bed. Squirts of oil hit my back and buttocks, causing me to flinch slightly. It wasn't cold. But it wasn't exactly warm either.

"I wish I could have made it fancier," he said. "Believe it or not, I'm a romantic at heart."

"Aww," I said, surprised to learn that about him. He wasn't the huge scary beast I originally thought he was back in the cave. Instead, he was a gentleman through and through with some odd tastes. "If you were to make it fancier, what would you do?"

He started to rub the oil into my back, his large palms warm and rough.

"A separate room with a real massage table. Flowers, candles, and candy everywhere," he muttered, his voice sounding thick with arousal as he rubbed the kinks from my shoulders.

"That's fancy for sure," I said, warmth flowing through my body at his every touch. The stress and tension between my muscles melted as he applied pressure on my lower back. His fingers pressing against my skin were like matchsticks, igniting my body.

"Does it feel good?"

"It does," I moaned. Then his hands roamed even further down, grasping my ass cheeks. My heart raced as he kneaded my bottom.

~

Seth

THE PRINCESS LOOKED sexy as fuck as she lay there, vulnerable and naked on a towel.

I had to do everything in my power not to fuck her senseless as I squeezed her pale butt, feeling her soft, doughy skin in my hands. Then, squeezing more oil on it until it was shiny, I rubbed her thighs next, wrapping my fingers around her legs.

Then I slowly spread her legs, and her scent of peaches wafted to my nose when I opened her up like a treasure. Blood rushed down from my head to the tip of my cock at the sight of her glistening pink pussy covered in slick.

I focused back on her ass, spreading her ass cheeks open and gazing at her puckered dark hold. Slowly, I ran my oiled finger against the creases of her tense hole.

"Do you like it when I touch you here?" I asked, pressing lightly against the entrance of her anus.

"I do," she replied hesitantly.

I spread her open wider and dipped my face between her cheeks. She was freshly bathed. The urge to lick her there was so strong it made my balls hurt. I licked her straight down between her ass crack, and she gasped loudly. But she still lay compliant on the bed, widening her legs lewdly for me as she laid on her belly.

She tasted so good: salty but sweet.

A thick, musky scent of peaches, which I inhaled like air itself. I licked her little asshole in circles, feeling the ridges underneath my tongue, tasting her.

After I made sure her tight hole was drenched in my saliva, I resumed rubbing my fingers around her hole. Then, very gently, my pinkie slid inside, stretching her. The princess looked like she was enjoying my play as I did that. The smell of her pussy intensified in the room with every thrust of my pinkie.

I removed my pinkie from her tight little asshole; then I quickly removed my jeans.

I lay next to her and pulled her on top of me.

"You're going to ride me, but turn around so I can watch your butt," I said.

She giggled as she mounted me, reverse cowgirl style.

Her fingers wrapped around my throbbing dick, which made it harder as she did that. When she finally stopped playing and inserted my cock inside her, I reveled being in her tight wet channel. She looked uncertain as she sat on top of me, my full cock stretching her out. Her pussy suctioned my cock as I grasped her hips to move her up and down.

"Just like that. Up down on my cock, like it's in your mouth, baby cakes."

"Okay," she said, squeezing her thighs as she bounced on my cock on her own.

I spread her ass cheeks and watched her brown anus flexing in front of me. I poked my finger inside her hole as she continued to squeeze my cock in her pussy, up and down. Her breathing was loud and strained as she was getting horny from my fingers. I pumped her anus with my finger and then inserted a second finger, stretching her further. It needed to be ready for my cock tomorrow. And my dick was much bigger than my fingers.

"Touch your clit," I said.

I needed her to experience pleasure while I was inside her. I wanted her to squirm and her pussy to clench with orgasms. I couldn't see what she was doing, but soon, her legs clenched, and she screamed from her climax.

"Fuck, I'm coming too," I shouted as she bounced up, tightening her pussy around my cock. Removing my fingers from her anus, I grasped her hips and shoved her onto my cock. My cock was deep inside as I exploded inside her.

It was amazing and magical having an omega for the first time in my life. Betas and other females would cry at a sigma knot. But not her. She quickly turned around to face me as my knot swelled deep inside her.

I pulled her face down to mine and pressed my lips against hers. Her body was lean and warm, lying on top of me while I knotted her.

"That was fun," she said, with exhilaration on her face.

"You just learned how to ride," I chuckled, pushing her wet hair away from her face. She was adorable when she was excited. "I could get used to this for a lifetime, you know."

"Well, that's good to know," she laughed.

Twenty-Five

LYRA

The next morning, I sat on the couch downstairs, watching as Kodan put a kettle of water on the old-fashioned stove.

"All we have for breakfast is coffee," said Kodan.

My stomach growled, and Seth to the right of me chuckled.

"That's not going to cut it for our omega," said Seth. He seemed to fit in seamlessly into our pack, and I loved that he felt natural around me. I wore my usual bathrobe, the rope cinched around my waist. His arm around my shoulders felt cozy as I snuggled next to him. Luke was sitting on my other side, watching the news on the television with his hand on my knee.

"I'll get us some breakfast," said Luke. Then he turned his attention away from the screen towards me. "What do you like for breakfast?"

"Anything you can find, honey," I said, kissing his scruffy cheek.

I walked towards the kitchen and pulled the fridge door open. It was virtually empty except for a large gallon of apple juice and a deer's head on a plate, staring at me with glazed eyes. *Ugh.* I shut the door, pinching my nose from the smell. Kodan needed to take better care of his kills or just get a separate fridge.

"Sorry about that," said Kodan, leaning against the sink and watching me. "Promise you this: we'll go grocery shopping in the city later today."

He looked embarrassed about not having groceries, so I decided not to give him a hard time. He'd already done a lot trying to fix up the place for us.

"I'll take a look around and try to find something," said Luke, throwing on his rain jacket and walking out of the house. "Maybe the mango man has something."

"Well, that solves it for now," I said, touching Kodan's forearm and running my fingers down the trail of hair to his wrist. He laid a hand on my waist, pulling me in close.

He was bare-chested this morning, still wet from his morning shower. He wore nothing but gray sweatpants.

I noticed the tent slowly forming under his pants from his erection. My pussy responded as my scent deepened. The pain from my heat had lessened, but it still left me horny this morning. Kodan guided my hand to his dick, and I gladly squeezed his large member.

His cock pulsed in my hand. My core began to warm, and tingles ran down my toes as my heart rate quickened.

Kodan began untying my robe hurriedly, and it dropped in a puddle on the floor. Seth joined us in the kitchen and came up behind me, kissing the back of my neck.

"Count me in, too," he whispered in my ear.

"We'll take her at the same time," said Kodan.

Seth smacked my butt, and I yelped, my pussy getting wetter with slick.

"I'll take her ass," said Seth. "Instead of my fingers, it'll be my cock in your tight little ass. Are you ready?"

I was scared but also horny at the thought.

"I don't know if I'm ready," I said.

"You can tell me to stop anytime, and I will," said Seth.

Kodan cupped my pussy and rubbed my clit with his thumb in a back-and-forth motion. My clit throbbed when he did that, aching for release.

Kodan stepped out of his pants, and while still in the kitchen, he lifted me by the waist, spearing his dick into my waiting pussy. It went in easier than before after being stretched out by all three of them last night. I flinched at the soreness of my pussy. When he slowly started to thrust and move inside me, the ache eased up.

I arched my hips forward to meet his hard thrusts.

Kodan held my thighs up around him as I held onto his arms. Heart pounding hard, I felt Seth's hands on my butt, spreading my cheeks apart. His thumb inspected my asshole region, and I froze up.

"Relax for Seth," said Kodan, bringing his mouth to my breast, sucking on it, and swirling his tongue around my nipple. His action forced me to relax as a wave of arousal pooled in my belly. He sucked each breast, his mouth clamping tight on my nipples.

Seth's finger pushed into my anus, warming me up before his cock invaded me. I pressed my lips against Kodan's upper arm. Seth was relentless with my butt, and he would take it one way or another.

He rubbed my anus with his thumb, arousing me further and loosening up my hole.

All of a sudden, a wave of warmth filled my ass, overwhelming me with need. I craved something inside it.

Then I suddenly felt something wet, and I realized that I had been able to release slick back there, too.

"You just needed the right stimulation," said Seth proudly, rubbing the slick around my butt. When he stuck a second finger in, the tightness disappeared, and I could feel myself stretching for him. I was allowing him in.

Kodan lifted me higher on his cock, pumping inside me relentlessly.

"Please put your cock inside me," I pleaded with Seth. I needed him to fill me up, too. I wanted both of them inside me. My inner omega wolf was desperate.

"Where, Princess?" asked Seth, knowing full well what I meant.

"In my ass," I gasped as Kodan flicked my clit with his finger.

Seth's cock was thick against my entrance as he slowly worked his way inside me, filling me inch by inch. My ass clung tight to his dick when he inserted himself inside me. It was thrilling to feel both cocks inside of me, pulsing and pounding in me. Seth started slowly at first, pushing in and out in gentle thrusts. But when I pushed my butt out further to him, he increased his speed, matching Kodan's rhythm.

Everything felt so hot and so forbidden.

"Flex for me," ordered Seth.

I tightened the pressure of my anus around his dick, and he groaned, his hands holding my ass cheeks wide open.

As I bounced in the air between them, both cocks angry, and inside of me, I couldn't help but wonder how any of my princess training prepared me to be ravaged by two intense sigmas. I felt like a rag doll between them, used and needed by these males.

Their sigma strength didn't wear out as they held me up between them, pumping their cocks inside me.

The kettle started to screech as the water boiled.

Kodan reached behind him to turn it off. I giggled, but as soon as he finished fumbling to turn it off, he turned back to me with a half smile, pistoning straight inside my pussy.

My stomach muscles clenched as I felt an intense warmth

in my womb. I could feel my release coming. I dug my fingers into Kodan's arms and screamed as the climax crashed through my body, causing me to see stars. He roared, his cock pulsing powerfully inside me, knotting and releasing hot liquid inside my womb as I lay limply against him. Seth followed suit soon after, also exploding inside me, trapping me against his knot.

My holes felt full and stretched to my limits as they carefully walked me to the living room rug, laying me between them. Being sandwiched between the two of them felt amazing as I rubbed on Kodan's chest, and Seth kissed my shoulders from behind, spooning me.

"I decided that in the future, we'll buy you a proper house back in the main city with everyone else. Nearer to your family," said Kodan out of nowhere.

"We don't have to do that," I said.

"What? That's all you've been saying," said Kodan. "Are you saying you want to stay here in the mountains?"

His face lit up, and my smile widened.

"We can stay out here, but in a bigger home. I like being closer to nature, away from the city."

"But your makeup studio dream..."

"I can work on that here," I said. I had grown to love being out here in the quiet. There weren't many people calling my phone or needing my attention constantly.

"Are you sure?"

"Yes," I said. "But now and then, I'd like to visit my family and friends."

"Of course," said Kodan, smiling. "Thank you for not moving me away from the mountains."

"I know."

"Shit, I would take the city life any day," said Seth. "My brother doesn't know what he's talking about."

"If I can't handle the mountain life, we'll go to the city," I laughed, trying to wiggle my ass, but couldn't because of his knot still inside of me.

The front door opened, and Luke's eyes widened upon seeing me knotted in both ends. Then, locking the door behind him, he rushed over with a paper bag in his hands.

"Princess, are you okay?" he asked me, looking daggers at both brothers.

"I'm okay," I said.

"Did you ask for this?"

"I mean, it just happened this way," I said. His eyes narrowed, and I knew I had to calm him right away. "Remember, they're my mates too. I feel perfectly fine."

"Listen, Mr. Alpha," said Seth. "If we were alphas, you'd trust us, right? But because we're sigmas, you think we're uncivilized shits?"

"No...I," said Luke, stammering for words.

"Seth, leave it," said Kodan in warning, rubbing the back of my palm with his thumb reassuringly. "We can't get fucking worked up about this. Luke, we'll not question you if we see you knotted inside our princess. And you will not question me while I'm knotted inside her."

"Guys, stop," I sighed. They were being so ridiculous.

"Alright then. It's just weird because one second we were discussing breakfast, and then you're completely knotted once I left," said Luke, his eyes turning to the paper bag. "Moving on, I brought some breakfast."

"Ooh, you brought my favorite," I squealed upon seeing the chocolate muffins.

"I'll feed you, honey," said Luke. "You had a busy morning."

I opened my mouth wide, and he ripped a piece of the muffin, dropping it on my tongue. The delicious stickiness of the chocolate nearly made me orgasm all over again.

"Mhm," I said, eating the entire thing in five minutes.

~

LATER THAT DAY, we sat on the rocks at the beach.

I sat between Seth and Luke, watching the waves crashing against the rocks. The bottom of my dress got wet, but I didn't care. It was so calming and relaxing. We were going to go to the mainland for some grocery shopping later. But I begged them to take me here before the long ride.

"How did you stay in that creepy cave for so long?" I asked Seth, my eyes constantly darting in that direction.

"I didn't notice it in my wolf form," he replied, rubbing my forearm.

The boulder underneath my hands was cold, and it felt nice against my heated skin. My heat wasn't as bad as it had been. It had tapered to a manageable level, causing my pussy to throb every few minutes. But the horrible clenching feeling from earlier had ceased, thank goodness.

Kodan stood up from his spot and stood in front of me. His leather jacket flew around him in the wind as he stuck his hands in his pockets.

"Lyra, I wanted to thank you for your patience and commitment to me," he started. I smiled, completely taken off guard by him. "But something was missing at our wedding. Do you remember what that was?"

I thought for a moment.

"I don't know what you're talking about," I said.

Kodan dropped to one knee and pulled out a ring from his pocket. It was a simple iron ring that had the shape of a tiny heart molded on top of it.

I held a hand to my mouth in shock. He actually remembered to get me a ring to the best of his ability.

"It was a rushed wedding, so I didn't have time to get a ring," he said. I got up and soundlessly hugged him as tears fell from my eyes. I couldn't believe it. He chuckled, a deep rumble in his chest showing his mirth and affection for me. "Let me put it on you."

I released him and stuck my hand out as he slowly rolled it over my finger.

"It's so cute," I said, looking at the tiny ring. It didn't matter how expensive this ring was. I just knew it came completely from his heart. "I love you, Kodan."

"I love you too, little princess," he said, kissing the ring on my hand while still kneeling before me. "Don't worry, I'll get you a more expensive one back in the city."

Then he stood up and pushed my hair back from my face.

His lips pressed over mine, and my eyes closed as we kissed to the sounds of the ocean crashing against the rocks and the seagulls screaming in the wind. It was the perfect storm.

As my body melted into his kiss, I realized then I never wanted to part with any of them.

I had found my perfect pack, however imperfect we may be.

THE END

Bonus Scene! <u>Princess For The Pack: Bonus Scene</u>

Continue on to reading **Book 4**: *Betrayed by The Pack*, following **Vanessa's** journey with Jack (Jade's brother from *Auctioned to The Pack)!*

Thank you for reading!

Thank you so much for reading *Princess for The Pack*.

If you've made it this far, I'd appreciate it so much if you left a review on Amazon, letting me know what you think! It helps authors like me keep building stories for you to enjoy for a long time to come.

I encourage you to join my mailing list so you can find out exactly when my next book release will be and so you can stay up to date on everything.

Here's the **Newsletter** link: https://author-laylasparks. myflodesk.com/vjzpbzbm3r

Follow me on **Tiktok**: https://www.tiktok.com/@ laylasparks_author

Follow me on **Instagram**: https://www.instagram.com/ author_laylasparks/

Also By Layla Sparks

Howl's Edge Island: Omega For The Pack (COMPLETED Reverse Harem Series)

Book 1 (*Tiana's story*): Stolen by The Pack

Book 2 (*Keera's story*): Auctioned to the Pack

Book 3 (*Lyra's story*): Princess For The Pack

Book 4 (*Vanessa's story*): Betrayed by The Pack

Book 5 (*Jade's story*): Matched to The Pack

Book 6 (*Alana's story*): Knotted by The Pack

Book 7 (*Lacy's story*): Craved by The Pack

Book 8 (*Olivia's story*): Freed by The Pack

Dawn of The Alphas: Omega For The Pack Series

Book 1: Maid for The Alphas *(Breanna's story)*

Book 2: Promised to The Alphas *(Ruby's story)*

Book 3: Denied by The Alphas *(Carmen's story)*